MIRI OF SHENANDOAH COUNTY

THE DAMSELS OF SHENANDOAH COUNTY
BOOK V

PIPPA GREATHOUSE

CONTENTS

PROLOGUE

L*ate November, 1861*
The midst of the Civil War...

T*HE POST*...

Miriam Clarke moved slowly to her room with the post she'd just received. It was addressed in Burton's neat script, as she'd grown to expect. Her hands trembled so, it was difficult to open the post she'd craved so much. But surely... *surely* this meant he was still alive.

D*EAREST* G*OD*, *PLEASE LET HIM STILL BE ALIVE AS I* *read this!*

She closed her eyes, holding it to her chest before she could bring herself to open it and read.

My darling little wife, Miri,

I hold in my hands the letter that I received just today, in your own script. May I say how proud of you I am, my darling? I have thought of you all day today. I remember the very first time I saw you, sitting at the Restaurant at the Hotel with Lady Wellington, eating breakfast. Those blue eyes of yours mesmerized me. I thought you a young girl then; I hadn't the slightest idea you were eighteen.

The next time I saw you, you were waiting outside the station for the stage, looking so lost and so alone. I told Lady Angel that Lord Wellington wouldn't approve if I gave you a ride, but even as I spoke I knew I couldn't leave you there.

Yes, you were so much younger than I, but I knew even then I loved you.

These past eight years have been wonderful, my dear little wife; the day you agreed to marry me was the happiest in my life. Yes, you were young; some would say much too young, but even if I should never return home from this wretched war, the past years I have had with you have been perfect.

I wouldn't have traded them for anything.

Please know, my dearest sweetheart, that I have you in my heart; always.

There is much firing going on here at present. I must finish this so it can go out to you; one of our men is being discharged today and is carrying a load of letters home with him.

Please give the others my greetings. And if you see Henson's wife, once again give her my thanks; had it not been for her years of classes, you and I wouldn't be able to write to each other. I have no word of Geoffrey or Francis. It has been said they are on special duty. Henson, I saw a few weeks ago; he was well, although homesick. William, I have not seen for a very long time, but I know he will write Gracie as often as possible.

Goodbye for now, my adorable and precious little Miri. I keep you always in my heart.

Your devoted and loving husband,
Burton

MIRIAM PRESSED THE LETTER TO HER CHEST. SHE would write again to him this afternoon; perhaps two letters; perhaps even three.

Dear God, how she missed him!

F

our years later, Thursday, Feb 23, 1865

TEARS...

MIRI HANNER CLARKE KNELT IN THE SNOW NEXT to the grave of her late husband, refusing to even attempt to brush back the tears that insisted on flowing stubbornly down her cheeks. The bitter air that proclaimed the presence of winter bit at her skin. She had stooped down to pick up the Easter flowers that pushed their way up through the snow on the way, amazed at their determination to bloom in this weather.

Quietly, she said a prayer, and kissed the flowers, laying them next to his grave in the family plot at the Pembroke Estate.

"*I miss you so, Burton,*" she whispered.

The sound of footfalls crunching on the frozen snow behind her met her ears just before a hand descended upon her shoulder. Miri turned to look up. Angel Wellington stood by her, with a worn blue velvet cloak over her shoulders.

"Miss Hazel has breakfast ready, Miri. She didn't want you to miss it. She said to tell you both of us need meat on our bones."

Miri's large blue eyes met Angel's deep green ones, and she nodded. "I suppose it's good she looks out for us," she said, forcing a smile. "Are you going to the hospital today?"

Angel nodded. "I am. I must keep busy. It's hard to keep a cheerful smile in front of the children; they know how worried I am. We may stop by and pick up Merrie if she wishes to go. Even if she can't handle the sight of blood, she can pass out the cookies Lillie sends, and read to the men. Mollie went today too, but she's already left in the wagon."

A forced giggle escaped Miri's lips. "Oh, I'm glad.

I get such enjoyment from listening to Mollie lecture the doctors on the importance of washing their hands."

"Yes!" Angel was laughing now. "But Mollie has kept many a mother and baby alive with her clean hands. The doctors should be thankful for her advice. Even if they aren't, they should be. I hope to see Gracie and Ellie while we're there, too."

Miri's face suddenly became grim. "I'm sorry about the dormitory."

"Quite all right, Miri. I knew when war broke out, they would probably take it for a hospital. Perhaps when it's over..."

Miri nodded.

The dormitory wasn't the only thing the Union, currently in control of Shenandoah County, had confiscated. The church, including the basement, had also been taken. Some of the houses in town had been taken over by the infantry. Gracie Becker had been forced out of her home after William left for the war, and had moved in with Ellie, Sheriff Henson Andrews's wife. Their twin girls were six now, and even more mischievous than they'd been at three. Their older brother Thomas at age 12, was doing his best to be the man of the house.

Miss Hazel was waiting when they arrived in the

Dining room. Stout, and huffing and puffing, she nodded, glad to see them. "The children have eaten, and are back upstairs beginning their studies with the governess. Breakfast is waiting on the buffet."

Angel wandered over to it. Among the dishes stood the beautiful blue crystal lamp of which she was so fond. She ran her hand gently over the surface, and glanced at Miri.

"Miss Hazel keeps telling me I should put this away. Geoffrey's mother brought it with her from England when they sailed. It's just that I do love it so. It was her favorite piece."

Miri smiled. "And now it's your favorite."

"Yes. I wish I could display it again in the drawing room by the window. The sunlight always cast prisms of blue light all over the room, remember? But when the soldiers began getting too close to the house, I decided perhaps it was safer in here. I'm thankful Miss Hazel keeps an eye on it."

At the mention of Miss Hazel's name, the housekeeper appeared. "Lizzie is demanding to know if her Papa sent a post."

Angel met her gaze, her dark green eyes wide. "What did you tell her?"

Miss Hazel looked slightly sad. "I told her that her Papa has a war to fight—but he has not forgotten her. He would write as soon as possible."

Miri watched as Angel nodded, lowering her gaze sadly to the table. It had been two months since a post had arrived from Geoffrey. "Thank you, Miss Hazel," was all Angel seemed able to say.

"Eat, loves." Miss Hazel's voice was softer now. "I shall get the baskets of treats from Lillie for the soldiers." She smiled at them both and turned, disappearing into the kitchen.

Miri ate silently, as did Angel. But it wasn't long before Lillie appeared, bearing three baskets. "There weren't enough ingredients to send anything but shortbread cookies," she said quietly as she handed them over. "There are just too many ill soldiers, and sugar is less plentiful now. Please let me know if it is enough."

They each said a quick *thank you* to Lillie, then to Benjamin as he helped them into the carriage and whistled for the horses. His rifle, he kept close at his side.

He had brought the older carriage this time, afraid the newer one would attract unwanted attention, and had brought some of the older, less sought after horses to pull it.

They caught sight of Union Cavalry ahead on the road, and Benjamin pulled the horses back waiting for them to pass. Inside, Miri was watching from one window, Angel from the other. Miri's small hand reached instantly into her pocket, feeling the smooth barrel of the pistol that Burton had given her before he left. He had spent hours teaching her how to shoot, until her aim satisfied him. She wondered if Angel had brought hers along as well, but didn't ask.

The moment was tense; finally, as the carriage moved forward, she relaxed and found herself looking out the window. It wasn't long until she saw the small house she and Burton had spent most years of their married lives in.

Angel's hand covered hers. "You miss it," she said, looking out toward the house.

Miri nodded. "Terribly. It needs someone to live in it."

"But Miri, I'm so glad you're staying with us," Angel said earnestly. "I would have been terribly lonely if you hadn't moved into the house."

Miri swallowed and turned to her with a smile. "Thank you, milady. I appreciate it so."

"No. For the last time, call me Angel. No more 'milady.' You're my friend, Miri. You haven't been a servant there for many years."

Miri's smile was uncertain, but she nodded. After a moment, her gaze returned to the window. "Do you remember the trip we made coming out here in 1850?"

"When the highwaymen attacked us, and Burton

was shot? And we both ended up being kidnapped by Mrs. Grimm? Yes." Angel's mouth became tight for a moment before relaxing into a smile. "Life might have been very different had Geoffrey not found us when he did. We both stuttered back then, too, didn't we? And now, neither of us does."

"If it hadn't been for Burton working with me so diligently, I still would, I think."

Angel nodded. "He was a good man, Miri."

Miri nodded with a small sigh. "He was, indeed."

The horses slowed and stopped in front of the big house known as the Adams House. Merrie's beautiful face peeked out at them from the window, and a moment later, she came flying out of the front door to meet them with her blue eyes flashing.

Benjamin helped her into the carriage. She had fastened her hair back this morning at the nape of her neck, but her blue eyes were as vibrant as ever as she climbed into the coach.

"Good morning!" She looked from one to the other, brightly.

"Good morning," Miri greeted her, smiling. It was hard not to smile when Merrie was around.

"How is Katie?" Angel asked softly.

Merrie shook her head. "Oh, Angel. She asks me every ten minutes if her father has sent a post. I truly hope we receive one in a day or two, for her sake."

"And for yours," Miri said quietly.

Merrie nodded, meeting her eyes. "Yes. I wonder if they have gotten separated. Usually one or the other writes. How is Lizzie? Katie will demand to know when I return."

"Very quiet. Except when she's asking about her father."

Merrie looked from one to the other. "I wanted you both to know," she said in a low voice, "that we have been seeing a lot of Confederate soldiers in the area near the house. It wouldn't surprise me if they tried to take it."

Miri's eyes flew to meet Merrie's in alarm. "I've heard that there is a tunnel under the house. Do you think they about know of it?"

Merrie's eyes were full of worry. "Yes. You heard correctly. There is more than one. One tunnel goes a half-mile to the tracks. There's an area under the house that the slaves have been hiding in, as a stop toward the north. Miss Constance feeds them there, and allows them to rest, before they go through the other tunnel to the house further north, but I'm unsure exactly which one. The tunnels have been there since the house was built. Francis has never allowed me to go down there, and he threatened me if I did. He said it hasn't been used since the Revolutionary War, until three or four years ago when they began using it to go north." Merrie's gaze moved toward Angel. "I wonder if the Confederates *do* know. We have seen them four or five times in the past few days."

Angel leaned across and grabbed her hand. "Merrie, you must bring Katie and come to stay with us. It may not be safe there for you!"

Merrie leaned back against the leather seat, deep in thought. Finally, she nodded toward Angel, then Miri. "I'll check and see when I get home this afternoon. If they've been seen again today, I'll talk to Miss Constance and see what she thinks I should do."

๑๖๒๑

THE REST OF THE TRIP INTO TOWN WAS SILENT. Benjamin finally helped them out in front of the church. "Miss Hazel sent me with a list," he said, as he ushered them toward the church. "I shall see if Mr. Greene has any of it. Where do you wish me to wait, Lady Angel?"

Angel turned to Miri. "What do you think, Miri?"

Miri chewed her lip thoughtfully. "Behind the Sheriff's office? I'll go down to the dormitory and help." But she was staring down toward the end of the street as she spoke, her brow lifted in curiosity.

Miri suddenly caught both Merrie's arm, and Angel's, as she gazed down the street. "Look! What's happening at the Andrews'? Gracie is bringing stuff out onto the porch, and she looks quite upset. No. Let me say it again. *She looks enraged.*"

They all turned simultaneously. There were suitcases sitting on the front porch at the Andrews' house. The home that belonged to Merrie's parents' next door looked fine, but the Andrews three-story had the front door standing wide open. Gracie Becker was carrying things out, her long golden hair flying out behind her. Her eyes were a dark indigo, large and furious.

"I'm going down to see." Miri let go of them and ran. Angel and Merrie were right behind her.

A moment later, all three of them had reached the Andrews' house. Miri lifted her skirts and took the steps on the porch, two at a time.

"Gracie! What's happening?"

Gracie, dragging a trunk outside, stopped and put her hands on her hips. "Oh, *hell's bells*. It wasn't enough that the soldiers took *my* house; they're taking Ellie's, too!"

"Where will you go?" Merrie's eyes were enormous pools of vivid blue.

Gracie's mouth became a flat line. "I have utterly no idea. But we're not staying *here*."

"Well, I do," Angel spoke up. "You're coming to Pembroke. With the children. All of you." Angel's voice was quite firm. "Miss Betsy, too."

Ellie, who had come up behind Gracie, was staring over her shoulder, her chestnut curls bouncing. "Angel, we can't do that. You already have enough mouths to feed there."

"I'm serious, Ellie. The more of us that are there, the better. Miss Hazel said this morning to bring as many of you there as possible. There is room in the nursery for the girls, and Thomas can share the room with the boys. And there are empty rooms upstairs for you and Betsy and Gracie." Angel began to grin. "Shall I send Miss Hazel for you, myself?"

"Oh, *dear Lord, no.*"

Miri smiled. "When Burton was killed, Angel asked me to come into the house. No, let me rephrase that. She *demanded* that I move in. When I refused, Miss Hazel came after me and nearly dragged me over. Out of my own house! Trust me, you two. You don't want that." She looked from one to the other of them, and leaned forward, lowering her voice. "And if you have any weapons, bring those too—and ammunition? Don't leave it for the army to take from you." Then she straightened. "I shall go down and send Benjamin after you. Then I'm going to the dormitory hospital to see what I can do. Merrie? Are you coming to pass out the treats?"

"Coming." Merrie nodded, turning to go.

But Miri heard Gracie's voice behind her, as she and Merrie began to cross the street, saying,

"I swear. She's as *bossy* as *I* am."

The injured soldier...

BENJAMIN MET THEM WITH THE BASKETS AS THEY returned.

"I figured you would be back for these," he said, grinning.

"I'm taking them," Merrie returned, laughing. "It's the only thing I can do. I faint at the sight of blood."

Miri spoke quietly, putting a hand on the coachman's arm. "Benjamin, please go down to the Andrews house? Gracie and Ellie and the children need to go to Pembroke as soon as possible. And Miss Betsy, too."

Benjamin tipped his cap. "On my way, Miss Miri."

They watched him go as Miri spoke.

"It looks as if we females will be in charge of the house." Her eyes were sparkling.

⚜

THEY INTENDED TO BEGIN WITH THE DORMITORY. Merrie took the baskets and set two down inside the door while she began going from bed to bed with the third to say a cheerful greeting and pass them out to each soldier. It was obvious the soldiers adored her.

Miri, however, stopped inside the front door and took a deep breath. This was hard. She had been working in this building the day that the soldiers had come to get her and had taken her outside to identify Burton's body.

She shook herself mentally, and her eyes searched the room to see where the physician was. She spotted one four beds down, who looked up to see her. There was no greeting; only a nod of recognition.

Miri turned to the right and grabbed an apron, putting it on over her gown, and then quickly braided her long blonde hair so it would be out of her way. Her face was pale. She had promised, after Burton died, that she would do whatever she could to help in the war effort, whether the soldiers were Union or

Confederate. It made no difference to her what side of the war they were on.

Brothers were fighting brothers in this war.

"I'm glad you're here, Miri," said a deep voice nearby. "A new batch of injured soldiers came in during the night. Some of them had to have amputations. Did any of the other girls come with you today that can help with nursing?"

Miri looked up into the face of Dr. Foster, who stared down at her. He looked weary; his gray hair was disheveled and his eyes more gray than blue. He looked as if he had been up all night.

"Hopefully, sir. Two of our close friends had their homes taken from them and Angel is trying to find them a place to stay. After that she shall likely be back."

He shook his head. "We need at least half a dozen nurses here. But thank you for coming, Miri. You're a tremendous help. I always know I can depend upon you."

"Thank you, sir," she answered softly, her large blue eyes scanning the room. Some of the soldiers didn't even have a cot to rest upon; they were sleeping on the floor on blankets. She sighed.

Was there anyone in town to ask for more beds? Cots? Blankets?

The door opened beside them, and three more

young ladies came in. Jennifer, along with Winnie and Ruthie who had at one time lived in the dormitory were putting on aprons as Dr. Foster explained to them where to start.

Each of them quietly whispered a greeting to Miri, who smiled back. A few minutes later a few more young ladies came in to help.

The Doctor turned to Miri. "This helps a great deal. There is a patient who needs constant care today, and I would like you in particular to be responsible for him. We took several bullets out of his chest last night. You'll need to watch for bleeding and fever, and infection. And change the bandage when needed; at least once before you have to leave today. More, if you see bleeding. Come with me." He led her through the maze of cots and toward the right side of the room.

"Who is it?" she asked, following.

He stopped in front of a pallet on the floor. "Captain Nathan Alley. I worked on him for three solid hours last night. I cannot afford to have anyone undoing my work, and neither can he. You're the only one I trust to take care of him. He eased inward, between a cot and the soldier, and leaned down to pull back the sheet, exposing the chest of the man on the floor.

Miri stared down at the soldier's face. She took a

deep breath, seeing him for the first time. He was an extremely handsome man, with a chiseled face, a straight nose, and firm jaw. His dark hair curled, giving him a boyish appearance. But his face, even in sleep, told her he was in pain.

"I'd like to move him to the first bed available. It's very important to watch the bandage for bleeding. If it spreads, call me immediately. If you don't I might not be able to save him. And even then..." He paused and looked up toward the door, as Miri nodded.

"Good God, here comes Mollie. I'd better go wash my hands; it's the first thing she'll ask me."

Miri plastered a small hand to her mouth to keep from laughing out loud. This was not the place to laugh. But Mollie was busy, and in her element, going from patient to patient, looking them over. At the end of each bed, there was a small slate with information about each patient. Miri knew the slates had come from the Adams' house. She reached down toward the end of the pallet on which the soldier lay.

Captain Nathan Alley
36. Chest wound
Condition: Critical
N.P.O except for small sips water
Watch for bleeding. Infection. Fever.
Last pain medicine: 6 a.m.

Miri looked at the school clock on the mantle. It was almost ten.

She set the slate down and looked to see if there was anything she could do to make the soldier more comfortable, noting the pinched look showing his pain. Then she leaned forward and tried to reposition the pillow under his head.

He groaned. Her eyes widened, and she pulled back the sheet slightly so she could see the bandage around his chest. Who would be here tonight with him? She studied his face. The dark curls escaping his unruly hair matched the dark lashes resting against his cheeks. She reached out to brush his hair back from his forehead and rested her hand on his brow. He was cool.

"Is he feverish?" a crackly voice spoke from above her, and she looked up to see Mollie.

She shook her head. "No ma'am. But he looks as if he's in pain. His last dose was six. Shall we give him something?"

"Wait until he awakens a little, so he doesn't choke," Mollie said softly. "Then give him a dose."

Mollie moved on to the next soldier as Miri continued to study her patient. She wished she could move him to a bed, but she knew in order for one to become available, a soldier would have to die. Her brow creased in a frown.

It was an hour before he groaned again and opened his eyes. Miri lowered her gaze to his, meeting dark brown eyes with golden areas surrounding the pupils. They were squinting at her.

"Who are you?" His voice was a growl, and she smiled at him.

"Someone here to look after you. And you are?"

He scowled back. "I know who am."

"So do I." she chuckled.

"Then stop asking ridiculous questions of me."

Miri tilted her head, and her long blonde braid cascaded over one shoulder. It did not miss his notice, and he reached up to give it a tug.

Miri grinned, and threw her hair back over her shoulder, out of his reach. "I'm just attempting to see if you're awake enough for more medicine."

"I am. But keep it. Someone else will need it more." His eyes closed in pain; she could see it.

"At the present, no one does. So you may stop being a hero." Miri's blue eyes flashed at him and his dark brown ones opened, glittering at her.

"You're a *sassy lass*."

"And you're rude. *And I,*" she said firmly, "am in charge of your care. So *be nice*, Captain Alley."

"So you *did* know who I am. I believe I told you not to be ridiculous."

She rolled her eyes. "So will you accept something for pain? Or not?"

He reached out and took hold of her wrist. His grip was hard, and her eyes widened in surprise at how strong such a sick man could be. She tried to tug her hand away, but his grasp remained firm.

"Oh no. I have you." His voice was a growl.

"No, you don't."

He closed his eyes. "I can hold on longer than you. If I were stronger, I would show you, young lady."

Miri felt her eyes widen even more as she stared at him. Still, he held on.

Sixty seconds later, afraid she would hurt him, she stopped trying to struggle away from him. He opened his eyes once again. "Tired yet?"

She sighed. "No. I'm just afraid I'll hurt you if I pull too hard, and you might bleed again."

He stared.

She stared back. Finally, she sighed. "Captain Alley—"

"Nate."

"Nate. Please allow me to get you something for pain?"

He glared at her for a long while. Finally, he nodded, and let go of her wrist. "All right. *Go.*"

She rose to her feet and went to get the bottle of

laudanum from Mollie, who was standing in the doorway of the kitchen. Mollie promptly handed it to her, along with a tablespoon. "He held out longer than I thought he would. Men are such stubborn critters."

But when Miri had returned to his bedside, he didn't resist. She gave him a dose, and then returned the bottle and spoon to Mollie and marked the dose down on the slate. As she knelt once again beside him, he reached over and took hold of her wrist once again.

"Captain Alley—"

"Nate." His eyes were closed. "And you aren't going anywhere, sassylass." It came out all as one word, and she shook her head, smiling.

Miri let her hand remain in his grasp until she was sure he had gone to sleep. Then she carefully removed it and felt of his forehead, satisfied he had no fever.

She was checking for bleeding when Dr. Foster stopped by to ask how he was doing.

"Aside from being the most recalcitrant man I've ever cared for? He's doing well."

"I'm pleasantly surprised," he murmured. "I didn't expect him to awaken at all today."

A COOL BREEZE WAFTED THROUGH THE MAIN ROOM, and Miri looked up to see Father Michael, the priest from St. Mary's. His face was tired, but his smile genuine and kind, just as it had been since she had first known him.

"Good afternoon, Father." Dr. Foster greeted him warmly. "Have you come to pray with the soldiers?"

"I have, sir. I may no longer have the use of my sanctuary, but these are my people and they need understanding and care. And mostly, prayer."

Dr. Foster nodded. "We had several recent cases come in during the night, Father. One of them lies on the floor next to Miri. He could use your prayers right now."

Father Michael followed his direction. Seeing Miri, he held up a hand of greeting, and she smiled at him.

"Miri. You're so dedicated."

"Thank you, Father," she breathed. "So are you. And it's the very least I can do."

He moved over and took the slate, looking it over, then lowered himself to his knees and put a hand on the captain's head, and reached across him, grasping Miri's hand. When Miri looked up in question, he merely shook his head. "I have no more Holy Water, child. But God will understand." He lowered his head and in the humblest of voices, began.

. . .

"ALMIGHTY AND ETERNAL GOD,
  You are the health of those who believe in you. Hear us.."

MIRI HAD LISTENED TO FATHER MICHAEL PRAY hundreds of times before, but she was extremely touched as he crossed himself and rose.

"Miri, don't forget to take care of yourself as well, my child," he said, as he moved on.

It was three o'clock when Mollie came to stand over her.

"What is it, Miss Mollie?" Miri raised her head.

"We have a bed for him, Miri. We're moving him to it, and you can sit on a stool next to him. It will be more comfortable for you both. And you need to eat something. There is stew in the kitchen."

Miri nodded as two soldiers moved over toward them and picked him up, trying to move him as gently as possible. But his loud groan of pain forced her to close her eyes, hurting for him.

The move didn't take long. He was asleep again by the time someone handed her a small stool and she moved it next to him. Ruthie, nearby, gave her a smile as she began to check the bandages of the soldiers in the new area.

Just then, she felt a large hand on her arm. She looked down into furious brown eyes.

"You're still here. Go home."

"No. I'll stay until Dr. Foster tells me I may leave. And you, sir, can stop being so demanding."

"I'll be as demanding as I please."

"You're horrid." Miri's chin rose as she stared down at him.

"And you're defiant."

"You're sick, Captain Alley. I'm only attempting to care for you."

A powerful tug on her upper arm brought her down face to face with him. Miri gulped and took a deep breath. She felt her eyes grow extremely wide and uncertain.

When he spoke next, his voice was a deep growl. "Just wait until I'm well. I'll *show you* just what happens to young ladies who try my patience."

"Is that so?" she whispered softly, trying to seem brave.

"*That. Is. So.*" He punctuated each word strongly, staring into her wide eyes.

Miri was trembling; she hoped he didn't feel it. His continued stare into her eyes was piqued; hers was frightened, and she couldn't help it.

He released her, suddenly, and she nearly fell over on top of him.

Finally, she took a deep breath. "Would you care for a sip of water?"

He nodded after a few moments. "I am dry."

She reached for a cup of water, and helped him lift his head to drink it.

"Thank you," he said, in a whisper.

The words, spoken suddenly and so full of appreciation, brought tears to her eyes.

"Are you hurting?"

But now, the irritation was back. "No."

Miri lifted her chin. "I don't believe you."

Captain Alley turned his head toward her and scowled. "You, young lady, are what is commonly referred to as a *brat*. You could use some discipline in my opinion."

She grinned. "Perhaps in your opinion, but not in mine. But it's nearly time for you to have some more medicine." She paused. "Will you take it if I go and get it?"

"And what makes you think you know better than I?" He closed his eyes.

Her voice, when she spoke, was soft. "Because," she said, "You're gritting your teeth, and it is not just because you despise me. Your abdomen is rigid, and your brow is creased, and you—"

"All right." His voice was rough. "You may go get it. I shall take it, if only to get you off my back."

"I could go find Miss Mollie and get her to bring it."

"*Oh dear God, no*. Bring it yourself. I heard stories about Miss Mollie before you got here this morning."

Miri grinned at him, showing her dimples, and he stared back at her.

"Miss Mollie is really a wonderful nurse," she said. "You just need to get to know her."

His glare told her he obviously didn't believe her.

Miri put a hand on his shoulder softly. "I shall be back."

A moment later she had returned, and he took the laudanum without temerity. He put a hand on her wrist as she rose to return the bottle to the kitchen, and Miri glanced down uncertainly.

He was scowling. "And why should you think I despise you?"

"Perhaps it's not me, but my having to be here to take care of you, that you despise."

"No." He raised a brow and frowned. "Thank you for your care, Miss," he said quietly. "You've been kind to me today and I do appreciate it."

Miri smiled. She glanced down at the hand that held her, until he spoke again.

"How long will you stay? With me?"

Her smile vanished. "Until Dr. Foster believes you're out of danger."

A scowl creased his brow. "I see." He released her arm, and she left to go and return the bottle and the spoon.

"How is he doing?" Mollie's voice said behind her as she washed the tablespoon in the sink.

"Captain Alley? He seems stable. There's no fever present, and he doesn't seem to be bleeding. He's quite..." she said and paused, "irritable."

Mollie nodded. "Typical soldier. *No. Typical man*," she said, grinning now. "I believe tomorrow, Dr. Foster might allow you to move about to care for some of the other soldiers. But you'll still need to keep an eye on him. I spoke with Lady Angel earlier this afternoon. Benjamin took them all—Angel, and Merrie, and Ellie and Gracie—all out to the house, along with Miss Betsy," Mollie shook her head. "And of course, all the children. I'll be staying until late this evening, Miri. You may go home with me. But you'll need to eat something. Here is the stew I mentioned." Mollie brought out a bowl and spooned up a portion of the steamy liquid into it. "Sit down and eat this, and I shall see if you can take a small bowl of the broth to the captain. The rest of the soldiers have been fed."

"Thank you," Miri said, smiling, and sat down at the kitchen table; the same rough sawn table that had been in the room for years. Miss Louisa was no longer there. Her triplet daughters had come to get her when the war began, and had taken her home with them for the duration of the fighting. Miri missed her.

She glanced up at the painting that still hung on the wall. Angel had shared with her that the painting of the older woman with her head lowered in her hands praying, was actually of Mollie. It have been painted by Lord Wellington's mother. But Miri decided not to mention it. She glanced up at the older woman.

"Miss Mollie, you look very tired. Are you all right?"

Mollie stared at her for a moment. Miri half expected a bark from the older woman, but instead, Mollie shook her head.

"Just tired, child. The war has taken its toll on us all." She rose, and went back into the next room, and Miri quietly ate her stew alone. When she finished, Dr. Foster put his head into the room.

"Take some to the captain, Miri. But only the broth. In case it decides not to stay down, he needs something light."

"Yes, sir. I'll do it now."

But when she took it out to him, he refused all but a few bites and growled at her, telling her to go home.

"I cannot leave until Mollie does." She growled back, tired of his irritability.

He raised a brow. "You stay with Mollie?"

"I stay in the same place she does. Pembroke."

He stared. "I know where Pembroke is. How did you end up staying there?" His tone was accusatory.

Miri, already tired, had had enough. "I'm there because," she said, letting her temper flare at last, "when my husband was killed in the war, I was alone, and had no place else to go. Lady Wellington and Miss Hazel both insisted I come to the house."

The captain's eyes were closed now, and Miri thought he must be asleep. Exhausted, she leaned forward and rested her head in her hands. She bit her lip as tears fell down onto her hands, and then her arms.

A hand suddenly, gently encircled her wrist. Miri didn't move, until his fingers trailed along the path of the tears that started at her wrists and went upward, touching her cheeks. She tried to jerk away but he made no attempt to release her.

"I apologize," he said softly. "I was being dreadfully rude."

Miri responded only with a slight shake of her head. She turned away with an attempt to wipe away the tears with her other hand. Still, he held on to her wrist.

"Your name, young lady." When she didn't answer, he spoke again. "I want to know your name."

At length, she turned back to face him. "Miriam." It was almost inaudible, and she added, "They call me Miri."

"I assume you have a last name, Miri?"

Her gaze was downcast now. "Clarke."

His glittering brown and gold eyes narrowed as he pulled her toward him slightly. "I'm in hopes, Miri Clarke," he said, softly, "that when I see you again, we can hit it off on a better foot. Are you in agreement?"

Her eyes met his. "Perhaps."

He looked tired; Miri waited until his eyes closed. But a moment later he spoke again. "Please, let me know before you leave, Miri."

"I'll try," she whispered quietly, "to awaken you."

❧ 3 ❧

S *nowing...*

SHE ENDED UP LEAVING AT ABOUT SEVEN, AT THE
urging of Dr. Foster and Mollie.

"Benjamin is outside, child. It is cold and snow-
ing. We must go *now,* lest we get trapped in a
blizzard."

Miri looked down. "Captain?" she whispered
softly.

A small moan escaped him as Miri checked his
bandage once more. Finding it clean she rested her
hand on his forehead; there was no fever.

"Go, Miri," Dr. Foster put his hand on her shoulder. "I'll see he gets another dose of laudanum when he awakens. You have done well, today. I hope you'll be able to get here tomorrow."

"Yes, sir, I plan to be here." She murmured, as she rose to go to the door. She took one more backward glance at the captain; he seemed to be sleeping soundly. Then she grabbed her cloak and followed Mollie outside.

"Benjamin brought the carriage for us, Miri, and some blankets. We both should have dressed more warmly this morning."

The wind was blowing as they left the building and allowed Benjamin to help them up inside. But Miri stopped before getting in.

"Have you blankets, Benjamin? To keep warm topside?"

"Yes, Miss Hazel insisted." He was grinning. "You need not worry about me."

"All right, then," Miri climbed into the carriage behind Mollie as he closed the door. She was already shivering. It had seemed warm enough this morning when they had left. The wind and snow blew her braid back, and she pulled the ribbon from it to loosen it; perhaps that would help warm her. But she couldn't help peering out the window toward Benjamin's lantern light, to see the snow that blew rapidly across the landscape.

"Mollie?" she spoke, alarmed, as they passed Merrie's home. "There are so many horses at the Adams' house."

Mollie's face was grim. "I know. The Confederates have taken it over. I pray to God that they don't do the same with Pembroke. Miss Constance sent Lady Merrie and little Katie to Pembroke, and some of the staff. Here, child. Wrap this around you." She handed over an extra blanket. "Your voice is trembling now. It may be fear, but you need extra warmth."

Miri took it obediently and wrapped herself inside. Leaning back in the seat, she couldn't get the image of Captain Alley out of her mind. His wound had been atrocious. She wondered if he would be able to return to battle.

And at the same time she prayed he wouldn't.

She was still thinking of the way he had held on to her wrist and had touched her cheek when she went to bed that night.

And prayed that he would still be there tomorrow when she went back.

❧

THE SUN REFLECTING ON THE SNOW THE NEXT morning made the world extremely bright. Miri forced herself to sit up and looked out the window to see how much it had snowed during the night. The family graves in the courtyard showed that the tops of the stones were barely visible. She knew which stone belonged to Burton, even from a distance and blew him a kiss. But she realized it was unlikely she would be able to get out that far in the snow.

Gracie's voice, from the other side of the enormous bed sounded drowsy this morning. She forced herself to sit up, stretching and yawning. "How bad is it?" she murmured.

Miri continued to stare out the window. "I think we might be able to get to town on horseback, but I doubt the carriage can get out."

"Hm. I'm so glad Ellie and the children—and Mrs. Williams—got here yesterday."

"And you." Miri said, grinning at her.

"I'm quite glad of that, too." A giggle escaped from Gracie. "You and Angel were a God-send, yesterday." She paused. "Are you still thinking about your soldier?"

"What soldier?" Miri turned toward the mirror, ignoring the question.

"Hm. What soldier indeed. Merrie told me about you being assigned to Captain Alley."

"Yes. That was Dr. Foster's idea, not mine. And he's not *my soldier*."

"Well, I understand he's quite handsome. Ruthie

told me about him. And she said he was very posses-
sive of you. And you, dear Miri, are still so beautiful
and so young…"

Miri threw up a hand, stopping her. "Actually, he
was a pain in the—um—"

Gracie giggled hysterically. "All right. But what I
said is the truth. And *you*, my dear friend? You
know it."

Miri laughed, turning back to face her. "Gracie,
did anyone ever tell you that we're never in doubt
about what you think?"

Gracie's face was rueful. "William does. Quite
frequently. He continues to lecture me for a half a
page every post he sends. I swear, I almost—" She
halted when she saw Miri's face. "I'm so sorry, Miri."

But Miri scooted across the bed toward her,
throwing her arms about Gracie's neck. "Don't be,
dear Gracie. I'm so delighted that Angel had us share
a room. I love being in your company."

"And I love being in yours. However, if I mouth
off too much, please promise to tell me."

"All right. But I've been so lonely, Gracie. You'll
cheer me up, I'm sure of it."

GRACIE HELPED MIRI BRUSH OUT HER LONG HAIR, as she wore hers, fastened only with a ribbon at the nape, and within a few minutes everyone was chattering downstairs around the dining room table. Merrie and Angel were sharing a room, as were Betsy Williams and Ellie. Katie and Lizzie occupied the Nursery along with the twins. Geoffrey Francis and Nicholas George now occupied the room across the hall with Abel and Thomas. Abel, who was also fourteen, and the son of Gleason and Kathleen from the Adams property, was looked up to by the rest of the boys, and everyone seemed to have settled in.

"Plans today?" Gracie asked as she glanced around the table. "I'd like to go to the hospital if we can get there."

"I plan to, as well." Miri nodded toward her.

Merrie looked up. "I want to go home for a bit and check on Miss Constance to make sure everyone is all right."

"That's dangerous, Merrie," Angel answered. "But if you're determined to go, take Sebastian with you, and keep him with you. He's just big and burly enough that you might be safe from the soldiers."

Merrie sighed. "All right, but I must know what's happening there."

Miss Hazel entered the dining room just as Merrie made her statement. "Lady Merrie, I shall go to check on Miss Constance and what is left of the staff there. You should stay here. Or go to the hospital."

Before Merrie could answer, Miss Hazel was gone.

"Remember, Merrie, she thinks of us as children, " Angel said, grinning. "Don't take her too seriously."

"And remember," Gracie said, in a low voice. These soldiers—some of them have not—um—you know—in quite a while. It sounds crude, I know, but I had to fight one off when they took my house. It would not be wise for you to go over, even with Sebastian."

Ellie sighed. "Perhaps I could go and read to the wounded soldiers in the hospital, then." She picked up her fork, but found herself picking at her food.

Miri was unable to eat much, either. She gave up on pushing her food around on her plate, and finally set her fork down. "I'll go out to the stable and see if it's possible to take the horses in. And I shall check on Mollie to see if she wishes to go." She stood up, and nodded toward Angel. "Please tell Miss Hazel thank you for the lovely breakfast."

The snow was deep, almost up to the top of her boots, as she trudged outside toward the stables. She stopped, staring outward toward the road. The Union Cavalry was passing by, making their way slowly through the snow. Several of them turned and tipped their hats to her as she stared across the yard. Miri raised a hand in return. When they passed, she moved on toward the right side of the house.

Benjamin saw her and came forward.

"Benjamin? Is it possible to make it to town today?"

He looked out toward the road. "Give me a half-hour, Miss Miri. I believe the Cavalry has knocked down a good bit of the snow. How many of you are going? Mollie left on horseback an hour ago."

IT TOOK ONLY A HALF-HOUR. BENJAMIN STOPPED with them in front of the dormitory to help Miri and Gracie out. Then another stop at the church to escort Merrie, Angel and Ellie inside before taking the horses down to the Thatcher's to shelter them in the stable.

Miri and Gracie found Mollie in the dormitory.

Dr. Foster met them just inside the shared room of the dormitory. "I'm thankful you're here. Mollie has already begun to change bandages and warm water for the soldiers to bathe. The ladies have had trouble getting here today."

"I'll build up the fire," Gracie offered, "and then help Mollie."

MIRI OF SHENANDOAH COUNTY

Miri had her apron on by the time the doctor returned.

"Miri, stay with Captain Alley as much as you can today. He's not out of danger yet. But I know Mollie will need you, too."

"Yes sir. I shall." She smiled at the elderly physician, thinking he looked more rested today. "Did you get some sleep, sir?"

"More than expected, Miri."

She moved forward to speak with Mollie.

"Your soldier needs you, child. His bandage needs changing, and I believe it is time for something for pain."

Miri turned to look for Captain Alley, but she did not immediately see him. When she finally found him, she frowned; he had been moved closer to the hearth. She wondered if he had been running fever and complained of cold.

She stopped at the end of the bed and looked at his slate. No fever, but they had been compelled to change the bandage once during the night due to bleeding.

She set the slate down and looked up to find him studying her intently.

"Good morning, Captain. How do you feel?"

"I'm here. It surprises me that you made it in. I was concerned."

"Don't be, Captain."

"Nate. And I believe, young lady, you were supposed to let me know when you left last night."

Her chin lifted defiantly. "I did try. You were asleep."

"Then you should have awakened me."

Exasperated, she scowled at him. "I don't believe, sir, that you have any right to make demands of me."

He glared back at her, studying her face. "I want you to do something for me, Miri."

She tucked the blanket in around him. "As soon as it is warmer in here, I need to change your bandages again. It says they had to do that last night."

"I leaked," he said. "Somewhat."

Her expression was incredulous. "Somewhat?"

"You're avoiding my question, young lady."

"It didn't sound like a question to me. A question goes like this: Miri, would you please do something for me today?"

Their stares at each other were full of challenge; His was irritated; hers, defensive. Their gazes clashed.

Gracie's voice interrupted them. "Um, Miri? Mollie wishes to see you."

Miri moved her gaze to Gracie. "Of course."

But the captain still had a fast grip on her wrist.

"Come back here after you see her, young lady. I'm not finished with you yet."

A sigh of exasperation escaped her lips, and he released her, chuckling.

Gracie turned away, refusing to speak. "No way am I getting involved in this," she muttered under her breath.

But when Miri returned, her hands were full of clean cloths and bandages. He eyed her suspiciously.

"And what are you going to do with that?"

"Change your bandages." She stared back at him, her chin lifted.

"They just did that last night."

"Yes, and you were bleeding. If I take them off to see your wound, I'm not putting the same soiled bandages back on. I'll use clean ones."

He nodded. "Ah. Proceed, then. And don't roll your eyes at me."

There was something in his voice that caught her attention. Miri stopped, before setting the bandages down. He was serious.

She took a deep breath and began to undo the bandages that bound his chest. With him scowling at her, her hands began to tremble slightly.

His hand descended on her upper arm. This time his voice was very soft.

"Miri," he said, pulling her slightly closer, "Who takes care of you?"

The question totally surprised her. Her eyes flew to meet his in astonishment.

"What... do you mean?" She said, with a gulp.

A frown made its way across his face. "I mean just what I said. Who takes care of you? Do you work in the house at Pembroke?"

She shook her head. "I did, once. As a scullery maid. Then I married, and we lived in a cottage out on the lands at Pembroke and farmed it. Until—" She stopped, and her gaze fell.

"But what I want to know is, who do you go to now, when you're sick? Or frightened? Or sad?"

She glanced down at his hold on her arm. "I—" she paused with a gulp. "I barely know you, sir. I cannot discuss these things with you."

"Then think about them." He searched her face. "I worry about you."

Miri managed a small smile. "You need not worry about me, sir. I'm fine."

He stared at her a moment and said, after a long pause, "Of course you are."

She glanced down at the pile of clean linen strips in her arms, and he released her.

"Does your family know you're injured, sir?" she

asked as she began to undo the bandages wrapping his chest. "I could write to them for you."

The angry stare that met her was equally as surprising as his former question. Miri's eyes widened. They stood there, gazes locked, until he finally leaned his head back on the pillow. "There is no one to write," he said, "anymore."

She stopped. "I'm so sorry, Captain—"

"Don't you dare to look at me with pity in your eyes, young lady. Injured or not, I'll bend you over my knee and smack you for it."

Miri stood up straight and put her hands on her hips. "Apparently, Captain, *you* don't know the difference between pity and sympathy."

He eyed her with a narrowed gaze. "To me they are one and the same."

"Well, *not* to me. And if you're incapable of telling the difference, you have no right to judge." Angrily, she pulled away one of the strips from his chest, more firmly than she intended, and when she heard the sharp intake of his breath, she caught herself. "Oh! *I'm sorry!* I didn't intend to hurt you."

He gave her a rueful smile. "I very likely deserved it."

She shook her head. "No one deserves to be hurt. I promise to be more careful."

"Thank you."

She stared at him for a moment before continuing. But after seeing the wound, she covered it and went to find Dr. Foster.

"I thought you might like to see his chest sir, while I'm changing the bandage."

The elderly physician followed her over. When he saw the wound, he nodded.

"I'm pleased, Captain. Apparently, the bleeding from last night was superficial. You're healing nicely."

The captain looked up. "Then I can get back to my men soon?"

There was an extended pause before the Doctor answered. Finally, he gave a long sigh. "Captain, I can't promise you that. I would be going against my conscience if I made any such recommendation."

Glittering brown eyes stared back at him. "You cannot be serious."

Sadly, Dr. Foster looked down at him. "I'm *entirely* serious, Captain Alley. You're healing very well on the outside, but I saw the inside, remember? You have more stitches in you than a..." He paused. "In a few months, Captain, you shall be good as new, but not for a while."

Miri, between them, glanced carefully from one to the other. Finally, Dr. Foster nodded to her. "You may finish bandaging, Miri." He moved down toward another bed.

Nathan Alley leaned his head back into the pillow, his face filled with dismay. "A few months..." he muttered under his breath. "*Dear God, what shall I do until then?*"

4

S*ympathy...*

MIRI LAY IN BED THAT NIGHT LISTENING TO Gracie's chatter without hearing a word she was saying. She was seeing Captain Alley's disheartened expression and hearing his words. He had not said another word while she continued to wrap his chest in the bandages and cover him up. Finally, she had put a small hand on top of his.

At first he had not seemed to notice, but after a few moments he had covered her hand with his. The difference between the sizes of their hands was astounding; his so large and hers so small. Miri

looked sadly down, and then met his eyes, hoping he
didn't notice her tears.

The captain's eyes crinkled slightly at the corners.
"Sympathy?" he asked.

"Sympathy," she repeated.

He raised a hand to her face and brushed back her
tears. "Don't spend your tears on me, little Miri," he
breathed. "I have broad shoulders. I'll be all right."

But Miri gazed into his eyes, her own big pools of
blue.

"I shall spend them where I please, Captain," she
whispered. "*I'm truly sorry.*"

He looked away, but captured her other hand in
his, holding it for a long time before his eyes closed
and she realized he was asleep.

He wasn't very talkative the rest of the day. Miri
didn't know what to say, and he was deep in thought.
But when she sat down by him on several occasions,
he touched her hand or her arm. Miri thought it was
only because he needed comfort; she wished desperately that she knew something to say to make him
feel more cheerful. But there seemed to be nothing
left to say.

She realized as she lay there in the darkness that
night, that Gracie had suddenly become quiet, and
raised up on one elbow to look at her. Gracie had
fallen asleep in the middle of a sentence, and Miri

grinned. Turning over, she looked out the window on the back of the wing, as she often did at night, facing Burton's gravesite. But it occurred to her she'd barely thought of him at all for the past two days.

Guilt washed over her. She'd been so concerned for Captain Alley, she had barely even thought of the dear husband whom she had grown to love so deeply. The picture of them on their wedding day glinted in the firelight from the hearth.

Slowly, she got out of bed and tiptoed over to the photograph, holding up the frame to see it in the firelight.

Had it really been so long ago when she had stood beside him? Burton had been so dedicated to her. He'd attended the local classes himself taught by Ellie, before helping Miri learn to read and write; he'd worked with her on the stutter, to help her have more self-confidence. She smiled, as she remembered his calm voice saying, repeatedly, "Think about what you want to say, sweetheart. Go over it in your head, and take a deep breath. Then try."

Burton had been utterly wonderful.

Knowing she would never find anyone as dedicated to her as Burton had been, she padded back to the bed and climbed in. Carefully she climbed down into the covers, determined not to disturb Gracie.

And slept.

※

IT WAS THE NEXT MORNING. SOMEONE WAS shaking her, and Gracie's voice finally disturbed her sleep.

"Miri, wake up! You must be dreaming of your captain."

Her eyes fluttered open.

"What?"

Gracie let out a delighted giggle. "I saw the way he looked at you yesterday. Did you think I didn't?"

Miri scowled, and Gracie laughed again.

"And you were smiling in your sleep."

"Perhaps I was dreaming about Burton. I went to sleep last night thinking of him."

Gracie's face became serious. "Well? Were you?"

Miri stared at her. "*No.*"

A delighted giggle pierced the air. "Well, there you are, then. Get up, my friend. It's after seven."

Miri pushed herself up and sat on the side of the bed with a sigh.

A few moments later, all the ladies gathered downstairs to eat breakfast. Miss Hazel came into the room, looking from one to the other, studying them.

"Miss Constance is sending more of the staff from the Adams' house here, Lady Adams. But she still refuses to come herself."

Merrie nodded, frowning. "It worries me that she's determined to stay there. Especially alone."

"Would you like me to go over and speak with her again?"

Merrie nodded eagerly. "Would you please, Miss Hazel? She's much more likely to listen to you than me."

The older woman nodded. "I shall do my best. And there is one more matter." Her gaze suddenly was on Miri. "I understand there is a captain in the hospital who will not be able to return to duty."

Miri sucked in her breath as she looked up at Miss Hazel with widened eyes. "Y-yes, ma'am."

"Don't stutter, my girl. You've not done that for a long time. But tell your soldier that we have an empty cottage for him to recuperate in. If he accepts it, he's welcome to stay here as long as needed. But if he would consider it, he could even stay in the house. It's dreadfully empty of men at the present. The Union has been eyeing it. If he were here, he might be able to give us a bit of protection. Especially since he holds a captain's rank. They might possibly listen to him." She looked toward Angel, who nodded, saying,

"Yes, Miri. I discussed this last night with Miss Hazel. It's a wonderful idea."

Miri tried to remember what Burton had taught

her. Be calm. Rehearse what you want to say in your head. Take a deep breath. A moment later, she spoke.

"He's not my soldier, but I shall ask. If he has the slightest notion that we're asking out of pity, he will refuse. However, I shall do my best." She looked toward the housekeeper. "Thank you, Miss Hazel."

Faded blue eyes met hers, as Miss Hazel gave her a brief nod and returned to the kitchen. "Lillie has cookies made for you to take," she said, as she disappeared.

Angel turned toward Miri. "Do you think he might accept?"

Miri shook her head. "I wouldn't even dare to guess. He's so..." she chewed her lip, thinking. "So determined not to be indebted to anyone."

Ellie grinned and leaned over, resting a hand on her arm. "So like someone else I know and love dearly," she said, softly.

CAPTAIN NATE ALLEY, ABLE FOR THE FIRST TIME TO sit up in a chair next to the bed, looked down at the blonde-haired, blue-eyed girl on the stool before him who had stuttered her way through what she was to tell him. *Where had the stutter come from?* He hadn't heard it before. She must be nervous about what she had asked him.

He reached around her waist as she spoke and moved her toward him so she could speak more quietly.

When he spoke, his own voice was a whisper. "Where did this invitation come from?" His brow was creased and his eyes flashed. Miri's wide eyes stared up at him as she arched her back, trying to move away from him as much as possible. "And I swear to you, young lady, if this is out of pity—"

Her big blue eyes flashed back, suddenly. "And I swear to *you*, Captain Alley—*it is not*. Regardless of what you were going to say."

"Then give me another reason."

Miri lifted her chin. "It's for our protection, too— although it may sound selfish. There are no men in the house and the Union Cavalry has been watching it for the past week. We fear that they might try to take the house for their own purposes. There are some young boys there, fourteen, thirteen, and nine —along with many other children who feel they are responsible for everyone in the household since their fathers are away. We have two or three grooms who were unable to go to war, but they stay in the stable. Geoffrey Francis and Nicholas George, and Thomas, and now Abel—would not hesitate to try to stand up to the soldiers on our behalf if they thought we were being threatened. And there are many other little girls, as well."

He reached out, lifting her chin further, and searched her eyes.

"Who do these children belong to?"

Miri frowned, meeting his eyes. "Does it matter?"

"Are they yours?"

Unable to understand his motive in asking, she scowled back at him.

"W-why?"

"Because I want to know."

Her blue eyes stared back into his for a long time, while he waited. Finally, she shook her head. "No. The ones I spoke of belong to Angel and Ellie—and Merrie."

"Dear God. And you have *no* protection?"

She tried to lean back to escape him, but he cupped her face with his hand and held on. "Answer me, young lady."

She blinked. "Yes, sir. That's true. But..." she halted.

"Finish."

She frowned and looked around her as she lowered her voice and leaned toward him. "But it's not just their children. The house is full of children of staff in the other wing who are young, and whose fathers have gone to war. Until now we haven't felt threatened. But the Confederate soldiers took over Merrie's house, and she was forced to come to Pembroke. And Union soldiers took Gracie's and Ellie's houses in town just this week, so we insisted they come too."

"Where is Merrie's house?"

Miri stared at him. "It's the Adams house, west of town."

"I know where it is. Why did you not tell me this sooner?"

She frowned. "Because you're injured and unable to do anything about it. The thing we worry about, sir is that we're the refuge for everyone. If we're forced out, there is no place for any of us to go. We were hoping..." her voice trailed.

"Go on."

"We u-understand you're wounded, sir. We would not expect you to d-do hand-to-hand combat for us. But we hoped even your presence there would help keep other soldiers from trying to come in and..." She looked away and blinked.

Nate's gaze was forbidding as it rested on the young woman before him. Was what she was saying true? He remembered times when his own men had wanted to plunder the farmlands of local citizens. He had forbidden it.

"You mentioned a cottage."

She nodded, once again meeting his eyes. "You could stay there, if you prefer."

"And how could I provide protection for the house if I did that?"

"It... would be more d-difficult," she said, with a shake of her head at the recurrent stutter.

His hand moved until he had taken hold of the long golden hair escaping from the ribbon and grasped it. She tried to move out of his grasp, but it was too late.

His voice, when he spoke, was a deep growl.

"Miri Clarke, I shall tell you *this,* young lady," he said, tugging on her hair, to bring her face closer. "I shall think it over. But if I find out that you're misrepresenting the truth to me, you will find yourself face-down, over the lap of one angry man. And you shall find yourself quite sorry. Is that clear?"

Miri swallowed hard. "*Very clear, s-sir,*" she whispered.

He held her there, with her face close to his, for a long time, before releasing her. When he did she moved quickly away and hurried into the kitchen. He could see clearly she was trembling.

Gracie followed her quickly, arriving in the

kitchen to find her behind the door and leaning against the wall.

"Are you all right, Miri?"

Miriam looked up to see her and nodded. But she was still shaking. Gracie reached out and hugged her fiercely.

"I heard what he said to you. *Dear God,* he sounds just like William, when he uses that deadly quiet voice."

A tear made its way down Miri's cheek, and Gracie, giving her one last hug, turned on her heel and wandered back through the cots until she stood at the bedside of the captain.

In the kitchen, Miri gasped. She couldn't help but hear Gracie's voice. If she was attempting to be quiet, she was failing miserably. It was angry and carried easily to where she was.

"Captain Alley. I have one thing to say to you."

Miri couldn't help it; she turned, watching through the crack in the hinged part of the door.

Captain Alley's closed eyes opened suddenly in surprise. "I suppose you're going to tell me what it is," he said, staring at her. "And keep your voice down."

But Gracie's angry voice grew louder with each word. "I am. You owe Miri an enormous apology. You had no right to be so mean. Miri was doing only what she was asked to do. *How dare you!"* With that, she turned on her heel and stalked furiously away. Beginning at the other end of the room, she began to see to the needs of the other soldiers.

Nate was frowning as he looked toward the kitchen. He seemed to be gazing toward the kitchen door as if gauging the distance and wondering if he could get there. Seconds later, he attempted to rise to his feet. Managing to make it to a standing position, he stopped, his face pale. He was blinking, and breathing rapidly.

Miri knew dizziness when she saw it, and she began to run toward the bed, but a second later she stopped. Mollie was standing next to Nate on one side, Dr. Foster on the other.

"Lie down, Captain," Mollie roared, "before you fall down."

Nathan was staring at her furious face, now; he blinked, and his eyes began to roll backward. Miri's hand flew to her mouth. She ran toward them as Mollie moved upward, and Dr. Foster moved to the opposite side of the bed. Between them, they managed to bring the captain back further onto the bed. Mollie helped him to lie back down, but the captain was awake and glancing around the room now, and began to protest.

Dr. Foster was furious. "If you undo my three

hours of work on the inside of your chest, Captain," the Doctor said, glaring at him, "I'll have a word with your Commanding Officer." He waited for Nate's nod and reached out a hand to check his pulse.

"I need to speak to the young lady," Nate said weakly. "Miri."

"I think that may depend on whether she wants to speak to *you*. If you're determined to get up and you agree to rest, I'll have some corpsmen come in this afternoon and we'll get you back up in the chair. Until then? *Stay there.*"

Nate's eyes were closed, and Miri realized he hadn't seen her approach. She quickly moved back into the kitchen and peered at him through the crack in the door. She expected to hear Mollie's bark at him, next.

But Mollie didn't utter another word. She glared at him, but his eyes remained closed. Miri backed away from the door.

Mollie turned, and entered the kitchen. She closed the door behind her a moment later.

"Miri? Are you all right, child?"

Miri wiped her face quickly and forced a smile. "I... am fine, Miss Mollie."

"Shall I go back and have another word with him?"

Miri shook her head. "No ma'am. Honestly, I-I'm all right. I need to go and see to the other soldiers."

Mollie made no attempt to stop her as she left.

Miri began on the opposite side of the dormitory, near the front door. beginning to check slates, checking on bandages, checking to see when they might have their next dose of medicine. She tried not to look at the captain as she moved through the room; at the same time, he was awake now and she was very aware of his eyes on her. When she reached the end of the room, she turned to see that Gracie had passed over his bed without stopping, her chin high in the air.

Miri sighed. She could not refuse to care for him just because he had become upset with her. She took a deep breath and walked to the end of his bed, checking his slate.

Blinking, she said softly, "Do you need anything, Captain Alley? Water? Something for pain?"

When he reached out a hand toward her, she stepped back defensively, staring at him.

"I need *you* to come here," he said, pointing to the spot beside his bed.

Miri didn't move. "What can I bring you, sir?" It took courage, but she forced herself to look at him.

"Yourself. And you may sit down, right here." He said, grimly. "I promise not to bite you."

She stood there, uncertainly, and he reached out his hand once more. This time she took a gulp and moved a step closer. But as soon as she was within his reach, he caught hold of her wrist. Her breath hitched.

"Hear me out, young lady," he said, his voice gentle now. "I spoke entirely too harshly to you earlier, and I wish to apologize. I thought you offered a place for me out of pity, but I see now that was wrong. Your friend Gracie set me straight. And a house full of women and children should never be left unprotected. Please accept my apology. I was entirely too nearsighted in my thinking. It would please me greatly if you would forgive me."

Miri met his eyes this time.

"*I forgive you,*" She murmured.

"Thank you."

She gave him a small nod. "It is understandable, Captain. You're in pain."

"That's no excuse." He lifted her chin a bit and met her gaze squarely. "You have been nothing but kind to me, Miri Clarke. And I have been quite—" He searched for the word he needed.

"Hostile," She supplied it, in a whisper.

He nodded. "Yes, hostile. I would understand if you didn't speak to me again. But you asked if I needed anything, young lady. Your forgiveness is all I need. You have given it, and it is enough."

He gave her long hair a tug and released her.

"I..." she met his eyes, but hers were filling with tears, and he caught the wetness on her cheeks with his fingers. Suddenly, he pulled her forward and down against his shoulder.

The tears continued, and Miri's shoulders shook slightly in silent sobs.

The room disappeared; there were no soldiers, no nurses, no crackling of the fire nearby.. It was only just the two of them. She was leaning on his shoulder and he was holding her closely, gently. It felt wonderfully reassuring. She fought the urge to crawl up into his lap, but knew she couldn't for fear of hurting him.

"*Shh*, little girl. Please, don't cry. I'm utterly sorry."

"It is all right, Cap—"

"*Nate*."

She swallowed hard. "Nate."

"And I accept your offer, Miri. It is very kind of you all to offer me a place to stay. I only hope I won't let you down."

"You won't," she said, pausing. "Nate, I'm certain you won't."

She tried to sit up and pull away, but he held her

there a little longer, his right arm wrapped firmly around her, and his left stroking her back gently.

"Nate?" she whispered, a moment later. "I-I need to go—"

"Yes. But only after you're able to reassure me you're quite all right. Otherwise, I intend to hold you."

The room had returned. Miri could see Mollie standing in the doorway of the kitchen, but the woman was not looking at them. Gracie was two beds over, and completely ignoring them as well. Dr. Foster was busy with other soldiers. Across, on the other side of the room, Father Michael was praying over a sick soldier.

She gave Nate a nod and a small smile. "I'm—all right," she said, her voice muffled into his shoulder.

He smiled and tilted her chin upward. "All right, then. You may go." Bringing her closer, he planted a kiss on her forehead, and her face turned a shade of deep pink.

Nate chuckled, standing her upright.

"May I get you something? I shall need to check your bandage before long."

"No. I'm well for the present. Thank you."

Miri looked up to see Merri's mother Marilyn as she came into the room, followed by Mrs. Greene, whose husband still ran the General Store.. Each one carried a large pot of what smelled like chicken and dumplings, and the soldiers began to clap and cheer good-naturedly.

Miri and Gracie followed them into the kitchen, to spoon out bowlfuls and carry it to the soldiers.

Miri smiled. At least the captain would be allowed to eat something today.

5

*O*rders...

NATE SAT IN THE CHAIR AFTER THE TWO CORPSMEN showed up that afternoon. Miri had finished changing his dressing, and moved on to the next soldier. He watched, thinking how competent she was and a moment later, he winked and smiled at her.

She sent a smile his way just as the front door opened. It was as if she couldn't help smiling back.

A Union soldier came in and took off his hat, looking around. A moment later he approached Nate.

Nate saw him; his face lost its smile and became utterly serious. He glanced quickly over toward the next bed where Miri was changing a bandage, and then warily back toward the Major. He raised a hand in salute.

"At ease, Captain. I just came to check on you."

Nate nodded to him. "Major. I feel fine."

The Major frowned at him. "The Doctor thinks otherwise."

Nate glanced across the room, where Dr. Foster was listening to another soldier's chest. Grimly, he nodded. "So I've heard."

"I'm putting orders in the works for an honorable discharge for you. I hate it; you're one of my best men. But it could be disastrous for you to resume active duty. The doctor said you might return to it in a few months, but that's a long time. The war could be over by then."

There was a long pause before Nate finally spoke. His voice was deep, and suddenly became very low, as if he hoped Miri would be unable to hear.

"I understand, sir."

"Where will you go, son? Home?"

Nate glanced up to see that Miri was listening. She met his eyes and disappeared into the kitchen as if to give them a chance to speak with each other privately. He waited until she left.

"There is nothing to go home to." He said, almost inaudibly. "Perhaps an empty house. Who knows if it even still stands? However—the young lady who just left.. lives at Pembroke."

"Yes. I know where it is."

The soldiers immediately around his bed were all asleep. Nate looked around to see how private their conversation was before continuing.

"It's full of women and children, sir. They are concerned that the Union soldiers will attempt takeover. Dr. Foster has also expressed to me it will be months before I can return to duty. The ladies at Pembroke. have asked me to come and offer them some protection. Two of the ladies there have had their homes taken by Union regiments here in town; one by Confederates. The Cavalry has been hanging about Pembroke. If I could ask but one favor of you, sir, it would be to give express orders to the Union to leave it be."

The Major sat there for a moment. "I'm aware of that. I'll give those orders as you request. But as you know, I cannot guarantee they will follow them. If you hope to offer some form of protection I'm agreeable. But you must know, if the Cavalry does not follow my orders you're limited in what you can do. Especially right now."

"Understood. There is one more thing, sir. The Confederates have taken over the house of one of her friends. The Adams house. Do you know where it is?"

"I do. Thank you, Captain." The Major nodded and rose to leave, then stopped. "Pembroke," he said, thoughtfully, rubbing his jaw.

"Yes. That's where I shall be."

"A soldier came home this morning, from the southwest, discharged. He brought letters for some of the residents in the area. He said the owner of the General Store told him the ladies had gone to Pembroke."

Nate's brow rose.

"I shall send him this way if he has letters destined for it. And I'll let you know when your orders have come through. Good day, Captain."

The Major gave him a nod and a salute, and left. Nate lay there, staring straight ahead, and muttered to himself.

"So it's official," he said irritably. "Well, *hell.*"

MIRI HAD BEEN PEEKING AT HIM THROUGH THE SLIT in the kitchen door, her heart saddened. Perhaps the captain would rather go elsewhere. Had he a home? She watched him as he stared across the room, looking suddenly lost. It was the same expression he'd worn yesterday afternoon, when Dr. Foster had told him he couldn't go back to duty.

Knowing she had left the man in the next bed without a new bandage, she turned to go toward the soldier's bed, wishing she could go to Nate's instead. She had just reached the foot of the bed when Gracie nudged her.

"Let me take over, Miri. I'll go wash my hands." She nodded toward Nate. "Go. Check his pulse or something." She giggled. "That will give you an excuse."

Miri shook her head as she slowly moved toward Nate. Sitting down on the stool, she rested a hand on his arm. "Nate," she whispered, "I'm so sorry."

His gaze moved toward her, as if for the first time he realized she was there. He managed a smile and moved his hand to rest on her shoulder.

"Don't be, my girl," he said, softly. "I shall be all right. This wretched war cannot last forever."

"I used to hear that from Burton," she said, shaking her head. "He was killed the same year it started. Would it be rude of me to say I'm glad you shall not have to go back and fight?"

The corners of his mouth turned upward. "You've just finished saying you were sorry I can't go back," he said, sounding indulgent. "Which is it?"

"Yes, but it was because I knew you wished to go."

His expression changed. "The war has taken all our lives from us," he said, watching her face. "I've lost my parents since I've been gone. It was impossible to even go back for their wake. Where they are buried, I have no idea."

Miri hesitated. Was there a wife or a sweetheart? She wanted so to ask. A moment passed in silence before she worked up the courage, and her voice trembled as she said quietly, "Is there—anyone else to go back for?"

He lifted her chin to study her embarrassed face. "Are you trying to ask me if I have a sweetheart?"

She nodded and looked away. Her cheeks were growing hotter and she knew they were crimson.

He surveyed her face carefully. "I did, once, when I left home. I was smitten; she, apparently not as much as I. She wrote to me at the end of four months to tell me she was marrying someone else."

"Oh," she whispered. "I'm sorry."

His mouth quirked up on one side. "Are you? I was, for a year or so. Then I finally realized I was better off. If she couldn't wait for me a few months, she would never have waited for me for four years. And part of that may have been my fault. Perhaps I wrote about the war a bit too much, and it was more than she could handle."

Miri's eyes narrowed in disapproval. "If she wasn't willing to understand what you went through day to day, perhaps you *are* better off."

He smiled and tugged at her long tail of hair. "I need to keep you around, Miri Clarke," he said, grinning. "You're good for my soul."

She returned a smile. "How are you feeling? Are you ready to go back to bed?"

His slight nod answered, and she turned and looked around for someone to help. Dr. Foster was not far away, but when she reached him and looked back, she saw Nate was already back in his bed. His face was white. She rushed to his bedside, followed by the doctor.

This time Doctor Foster took out his stethoscope and put the bell to Nate's upper chest, listening for a few seconds before putting it back in his pocket.

"Well, you sound all right." With a glare directed at Nate, Dr. Foster was gone.

Nate gave Miri a wink. She returned a scowl, and he laughed, putting a hand to his chest to keep it from hurting.

But something in her spirit grew lighter as the afternoon wore on; was it the conversation they had shared? Or was it knowing that he was coming to Pembroke? She wasn't sure, but it was difficult to stop the smile that kept escaping. She felt almost giddy.

Once again that afternoon, the front door opened. Miri turned to see the Major as he entered and strode toward Nate. He was holding a stack of something in his hands, but she couldn't tell what it was.

Miri followed the Major with her gaze. Surely he didn't have Nate's discharge papers already? She frowned and intentionally moved forward to hear what he said. But when she looked up, Nate was scowling at her with a brow raised. She halted.

It didn't matter. She could hear the Major's voice clearly.

"These are the letters I mentioned for Pembroke. I wanted to bring them to you so you can deliver them to the ladies there." He turned to leave, then turned back. "Also," he lowered his voice, "I have given explicit orders to the Cavalry—and the rest of the men, to leave Pembroke alone. Let's hope they follow them." He sighed. "That's the best I can do."

"Thank you, Major." Nate nodded quietly. His voice was quite low, too. "I appreciate it more than I can say."

Nearby, Miri had heard, and scowled in irritation. When she caught Nate's expression, he was chuckling at her.

Her mouth became a straight line. "Don't laugh at me, Captain Alley."

"Come here, Miri." His voice was deep and gravelly. "Now."

Slowly, she approached him.

"Hold out your hands."

Her eyes widened, wondering what he was about to do. But she held out her hands with her palms turned upward.

"Here."

Miri looked down. There was a large stack of envelopes lying in her hands. She stifled a squeal as she began to rifle through them, excited. There were two from Henson Andrews to Ellie, and three from William to Gracie. The rest were addressed to ladies of the staff who worked at Pembroke." When she looked again, however, she saw none from Lord Geoffrey or Sir Francis. Still, she squealed with delight and turned, searching for Gracie who was right behind her.

Another squeal from Gracie caused the soldiers who were awake to turn. Mollie approached from the other side of the room.

"Posts?" she asked, quietly. When she was met with a nod she smiled.

"I'll cover for you, Gracie," said Mollie. "Take them into the kitchen to read them."

"Yes, Miss Mollie!" Gracie hugged her, then hugged Miri and Nate fiercely. Then she ran into the kitchen and closed the door.

Nate's grin at Miri was infectious. "I suppose that

means she's forgiven me for lecturing you this morning."

GRACIE SAT DOWN AT THE KITCHEN TABLE WITH trembling fingers, and opened each one of them, pulling them out. Finding the one that was dated most recently, she pulled it out first and read the last page.

WE'RE IN JACKSON, MISSOURI NOW, LITTLE BEAST, *just 8 miles above Cape Girardeau on the Mississippi. We lost some of our men, but gained some prisoners of war as well. The battle is over now, and I believe the plan is to go southwest. We're awaiting orders as I write.*

Henson is dreadfully homesick for Ellie and the children. And I need not tell you just how homesick I am for you.

But my dearest little Gracie, as I say in every letter, 'this war cannot last forever.' It will not be long before I can once again hold you in my arms. Please write soon, and let me hear your impish little voice in my head. I long to know how you fill your days. Are you still working at the hospital? Please tell me what you do, in detail. Are you able to continue your art work in town? I know you said money is tight at present. But when the war is over, I hope things will be different for you.

I look forward to your next letter, little beast. (Spoken with truest affection, of course.)

And of course, as I always tell you,..
Behave yourself. Be ladylike...
and watch your language!
Your loving and devoted husband,
William

Tears streamed down her face. Knowing he had been all right when he penned his last letter, she quickly grabbed the other two up and read them.

And read them again. *And again.*

A half hour later, she opened the door and returned to her duties in the dormitory.

Miri, stoking the fire, turned to see her. Noticing Gracie's radiant smile, Miri turned back to the hearth.

At five-thirty, Jennifer Gregory came in with Letty Scott to relieve them. Jennifer came over.

"You look tired, Miri. Benjamin is outside with the carriage. Merrie and Angel and Gracie are already waiting inside, and so is Ellie."

"Thank you, Jennifer." Miri turned, looking for Mollie, and immediately found her, two beds away.

"Go home, child. I believe rather than leave right now, I shall wait for Gleason to come by. He will have the coach from the Adams' house. Some of his older girls are working at the church across the street today and he will bring me back."

"Yes, ma'am." Miri turned to look toward Nate and found him crooking a finger at her. She moved closer.

"You look tired, little Miri. Go home. I'll be all right."

She looked up at him with uncertainty. "Promise you won't try to get up by yourself?"

He grinned. "I promise nothing. The longer I lay in this bed, the weaker I feel."

She stood there, scowling at him.

"Go," he said firmly. "Now."

With one last glance backward, she moved toward the front door and took off her apron, being careful to take the stack of letters out of the pocket. She wrapped her cape around her, along with a scarf and mittens. When she opened the door to the old parlor, she looked back to see him hold up a hand, and gave him a wide smile.

The carriage was full, and Ellie was nearly bouncing in her seat.

"Gracie said there are letters?"

"*Yes*! Two of them. Here."

Ellie had them open and was trying to read them by the street lamp before Miri even sat back in her seat. But when Benjamin closed the door behind her there was even less light. The carriage began to move, and Ellie finally gave up.

"I'll wait until we get home. It's too dark to read," she grumbled.

Miri's smile was rueful. "I'm sorry, Ellie. I didn't realize you were out here or I would have brought them out sooner."

"I can wait," Ellie grinned. "Impatiently, but I can wait."

"How are you all? Besides being tired?" Gracie looked toward each person in turn. "I know how Miri is; she has been fighting with her captain all day."

"And winning," Miri added firmly, as if she dared Gracie to dispute her statement. "And he's *not* my captain."

"Umm, right." Gracie rolled her eyes heavenward.

Angel looked tired. "Changing bandages, emptying urinals, feeding soldiers who cannot feed themselves. And so on, *and so on.*"

Ellie grinned. "I just came in to pick you up. I've been wrestling with unruly children all day. Well, the twins, that is. Thomas is a perfect little gentleman."

"I've been reading letters from home to the soldiers," Merrie added in her bubbly voice, "and I brought a book from home. I swear, did you realize all poets are morose? I didn't bring Edgar Allen Poe, of course. I was halfway through William Wordsworth's *Lines Written in Early Spring*, before I realized how sad it was. It should have been named *What man has made of man*, by the by. And did you know—"

Gracie interrupted. "Then what did you end up reading to them?"

"*Pride and Prejudice*, by *Jane Austen*." When Miri burst into giggles, Merrie protested. "Well, they didn't seem to mind. And they liked all the voices, including the hysterical Mrs. Bennett."

Angel nodded. "They were laughing *hysterically at her, too*," she said, grinning.

"Well, they liked it anyway, and at least it got them thinking of something besides sitting in a room full of injury and death, and wondering which of their fellow soldiers would die next to vacate a bed. Oh, and I read them a little of..."

Merrie chattered all the way back to Pembroke. By the time they reached home, the rest of them were relaxed and ready for dinner.

"L eave Pembroke alone..."

MISS HAZEL MET THEM AT THE FRONT DOOR AS they piled out of the carriage, huffing and puffing. "Miss Constance has temporarily vacated the Adams house with all the staff, Lady Merrie. We set up another group of tables in the informal ball room, and the house is nearly full. The two lower floors are full now. Their children are upstairs in the Staff wing. But, Miri, we saved a room downstairs for your captain."

Miri didn't correct the reference to her *captain*. She nodded, saying only, "He will be here as soon as he can. And the Major came to see him twice today. I thought I heard him say that he would order the Cavalry to leave Pembroke alone. But.." she trailed, frowning. "But he didn't at all seem to believe they would follow orders."

Miss Hazel's brow creased. "There is no room for the Cavalry here." She looked from Miri to Angel. "Lady Angel, is it possible that Miss Constance and I could see you and Miri in the Library after dinner? And Merrie?"

"Certainly, Miss Hazel." Angel and Merrie seemed surprised. Miri, at the other end of the table, only nodded. Just then, however, Miri remembered to reach into her pocket for the envelopes. "These are for the ladies here at Pembroke."

Miss Hazel smiled. "Thank you. They will be pleased." She looked up at the rest of them. "Supper is ready."

Miri watched as Merrie disappeared into the informal ballroom to see if the staff was all right before coming back to the Formal dining room. The rest of the ladies shuffled into the dining room and took their seats. Miri had to admit; she was hungry. After making sure all the soldiers were fed, she had not taken time to eat lunch herself. Mollie had scolded her for neglecting to care for herself.

Ellie had pulled out the letters and read them,

after the meal was served, and no one said a word at her lack of etiquette. The parchment was wrinkled, as if it had been wet.

"MY DARLING LITTLE ELLIE,

I pray you and the children are well. Are Polly and Cissy behaving themselves? I doubt very much they are. Even as I write, in my mind's eye, I can see them racing around the house and playing hide and seek, or awakening at three in the morning to decide to bake a cake and completely ruining the kitchen. Has Thomas grown much more? The last time you wrote, he had run out of the General Store to keep them from putting a snake in Mrs. Kinsey's carriage seat. Poor Thomas. They keep him eternally busy.

But now, my precious wife, I want to know about you. The last time you wrote, the soldiers had taken William and Gracie's house. I pray they have not disturbed you at home. How I wish I could be there to protect you and the children.

Are you well? Are you getting enough rest? You wrote you went daily to the hospital to help the soldiers who were wounded, and were writing letters for them. What a noble thing to do! You're truly precious, my darling. How I miss you!

This war has gone on far too long. It cannot possibly last much longer. If what I hear can be trusted to be true, we are closing in. However, I know we have thought so before. These five years have been an eternity.

I pray continuously God will keep you safe. I have no doubt you pray for me as well.

Please pass a kiss to the children. Tell Thomas how very proud of him I am. To Polly and Cissy, give my instructions to obey you and to help you in every way they can. And tell them how much their Papa loves them.

And to you, my darling Ellie, I send all my love, every moment of every day. Sometimes I feel you in my arms at night, and I dream frequently that I'm wrapped around you, with your head under my chin and your arms reaching as far around me as you can. Those dreams keep me sustained. When you sleep at night, I hope you feel my arms about you, for they truly are. Always.

They are calling. I must go for now, but will write again as soon as possible.

Know that I love you deeply, and long to be there with you as soon as it is possible.

Your adoring husband,
Henson

ELLIE READ IT AGAIN BEFORE OPENING THE OTHER one, tears of longing coming in streams now, and she blinked to clear her vision as she opened the second. It was much the same as the first. Finally, she put the letters into her pocket and ate. The other girls remained quiet as she finished reading.

"It is always bitter-sweet when one receives a post," she said, finally. "It's wonderful to know that our men were well when they wrote it, but it makes us miss them all the more."

"Yes." Gracie's warm smile met hers. "I believe I was worthless the rest of the afternoon, after getting mine from William."

But Miri was quiet, and Angel put a hand on her arm.

"You look tired, Miri."

Miri only smiled. "I am quite tired. It was an emotional day."

"Because of the captain," Gracie said, with a cheeky grin. "He's not the most *patient of patients*." When she met Miri's eyes, however, she mouthed a small "*Sorry*," and closed her mouth.

Miri watched as Gracie turned away and gave Angel a wink.

It was then that Miss Hazel caught Angel's eye from the kitchen.

"I think Miss Hazel wants to speak to us. Miri, are you finished? Merrie?"

"Coming." Each of them nodded, and followed.

MISS CONSTANCE WAS ALREADY IN THE LIBRARY when they arrived. She had not changed out of the traditional garb she wore at the Adams house, and was standing in the corner of the room, looking worried. Her brow was creased and her faded hazel eyes wore the same expression that she had shown every time Miri had ever seen her. Merrie ran to her and threw her arms around the housekeeper's neck, surprised when Miss Constance patted her on the back. Her normal bark seemed to be missing tonight.

Miss Hazel's worry was no less obvious as she clasped her hands in front of her and began pacing. Angel and Miri sat down in the leather chairs and waited, while Merrie leaned against the bookshelves next to her housekeeper.

"First, Constance has something to say." Miss Hazel was back in form.

Miss Constance stood straight, tapping her cane on the surface of the hardwood oak floor impatiently. "The staff was forced to leave today. I sent them here with as much food and clothing, and all the weapons and ammunition as we could find. Gleason brought them over with as many of their belongings as he could. And early last night he brought over the horses we had, and as much feed as he could. He knew they wouldn't be safe from the soldiers. The weapons were hidden; the soldiers did not find them. *But they did* discover some of the young ladies who worked at the house."

Merrie's hand flew to cover her mouth as Miss Constance continued. "The girls are all right, but they were frightened out of their wits. I went after the offending soldiers with my cane, and they shoved me down. It was then I realized I couldn't stay, either." She turned to face Merrie, who was aghast at what had happened. "And, milady, we also brought over the gold, so they wouldn't find it and take it from you."

Merrie nodded vigorously. "Thank you, Miss Constance. It was thoughtful of you to remember."

"Of course we would remember," Miss Constance gave off her regular, gruff tone of voice, and then once again leaned back next to Merrie, who reached out and hugged her. Merrie knew by now how to see past the gruff façade that her housekeeper exuded.

Miri, concerned, looked toward her. "Are you truly all right, Miss Constance?"

"I'm all right. The girls are all right, now they have calmed down. They were not violated. It stopped when I came in, but that's when I knew we couldn't stay." She looked toward Miss Hazel, who spoke quietly.

"This is why we wished that only you three meet with us. Miri, your captain does not even need to know this." When Miri nodded, she turned her gaze to Angel. "We don't plan to touch the gold. With what we have in the vault, and if we're careful, we shall have enough to buy food and supplies. But no one must know about this."

Merrie's immediate response was to put up a hand. "But of course we will contribute to the budget for food and supplies. Francis would be quite upset if we didn't.

Miri spoke up. "And have we enough to feed everyone in the house?"

Angel's voice was soft and concerned. "I expect we do if we're frugal. It would be better if it were not bandied about town that the staff and weapons from 'the Adams house is here. I don't know how we can get as many supplies as we need from Mr. Greene without someone noticing. Miri, have you ideas?"

Miri raised her head at this. "We might perhaps spread it out. We already make trips to town every day. We can take turns passing the supply lists to Mr. Greene. I could make a schedule for us to take the lists and the gold in to him, and Benjamin can take the carriage around the back of the store to pick the supplies up. One of the three of us can take the lists in. And if we need extra, Kathleen and Gleason could occasionally make a trip to pick up a load since they are here now."

"I'm so glad they're here," Merrie nodded. "Especially little Abel."

Miss Constance's face broke out into an uncharacteristic grin as she said gently, "*Little* Abel is fourteen, milady, and taller than you. But he has already been trying to show the twins places to hide in case the soldiers come here. And teaching them how to be silent." Appreciation twinkled in Miss Constance's eyes, showing her fondness for the boy.

Miri smiled. She knew the story of Abel's birth and how Merrie had been ordered by Mollie to help deliver him when he was born. The next day she had gone into their burning house to rescue him. Abel had a special place in Merrie's heart.

"Back to the plan," Miss Hazel's voice was again her usual gruff tone. "You will take care of this, Miri?"

"I shall be glad to, Miss Hazel. If you will give the lists to me of what you need, I'll set up a rotation schedule for the delivery of the lists to Mr. Greene. We can change it up daily to avoid notice."

"It's a good plan, Miri," Angel said warmly. "And I'm glad your soldier will be coming."

"He has agreed to come?" Miss Hazel's gaze moved to rest on Miri.

"Yes, ma'am. But when he can be released from the hospital, I have no idea."

"All right. Thank you all. Miri, I shall get the lists

to you. And we give the payment for it to whomever delivers it that day."

Miri nodded. "Yes ma'am." She rose from her chair, with altogether too much resting on her shoulders. "I shall begin tomorrow to put things into place."

Upstairs, she sat down and made out the list for the next few weeks. But she ended up going to bed earlier than usual and fell asleep quickly even with Gracie's chatter filling the room. A few minutes later, Gracie was asleep as well.

THE AFTERNOON SUN WAS FLEETING; THE SHADOWS through the dormitory windows had grown long. Miri had been extremely busy working in the hospital all day long, once again missing her lunch, and her shoulders were drooping. She would be glad to get back to Pembroke, to rest. If Burton was only home to rub her shoulders and soothe her.

If only.

She was bandaging the shoulder of the soldier nearest the door when Dr. Foster came up and put a gentle hand on her shoulder.

"Miri, someone wants to see you in the front parlor," he said softly. "I'll finish this for you."

Her head came up at that; with trepidation, she met his eyes. They had a sadness about them. She moved toward the old room once used as the parlor of the dormitory and opened it. A soldier met her, his face grim.

"Mrs. Clark," he said, nodding.

"Yes?"

"Please come with me. I need to see if it is possible for you to identify..."

Identify.

It was the last thing she heard. Her heart sank. Her breathing became rapid and shallow, and she reached up and put her hand on his arm.

"Sir," her voice hitched. "Is it Burton?"

He gave her a sympathetic smile and put an arm around her, but said nothing as he ushered her outside. There was a wagon waiting just a foot off the sidewalk.

Miri gasped, putting her hand to her mouth and beginning to feel the need for air; she felt her eyes grow wider. There was a body in the back of the wagon, tall, with broad shoulders and covered with a blanket.

"Ma'am, I'm sorry, but we need identification. Please?"

She gulped, nodding, and he reached slowly, *slowly*

forward, to inch down the blanket from the head of the man she knew to be dead.

It mustn't be Burton. *Please, dear God, not Burton!*

Miri screamed and backed away as she saw the face of the dead man in the wagon. It did not belong to Burton.

It was the face of Captain Nathan Alley.

7

A *larm...*

"MIRI! WAKE UP!" GRACIE WAS SHOUTING IN THE midst of the screaming and pandemonium that suddenly shook Pembroke's third floor of the wing. "Wake up! You're dreaming!"

A lantern was lit in the room, and Miri finally witnessed what was happening through her already-open eyes. Breathing heavily, she stared into the face of Gracie, who still grasped her by the shoulders. She blinked.

"Miri, talk to me! What was it?"

Miriam stared at her and held her breath for a

moment; then she covered her face with her hands and began to sob.

Gracie threw her arms around her. "Shh. Shush, Miri. It was a *dream*. It didn't really happen."

Slowly, Miri began to calm. When she raised her head, she saw Merrie, Angel, and Ellie all sitting on the bed around her. Merrie leaned forward to put an arm around Miri's shoulders.

"Was it Burton?" she asked in a whisper.

Miri closed her eyes and leaned her head over on Merrie's shoulder. "I—I thought so, at first..."

"No?" Ellie's soft voice asked next.

Miri shook her head. When she said nothing else, Angel reached out, her eyes wide.

"*Miri?*" she whispered, "*Who was it?*"

But Miri couldn't bring herself to answer. All she could do was rest her head on her arms, hugging her knees to her. The room became silent.

No one else dared to ask.

The other girls, one by one, drifted off to their beds and left Gracie and Miri to talk. It was quite a long time before Gracie coaxed Miri to opening up and explaining the terror of the dream.

It was well after three before they had both gone back to sleep.

Gracie...

The sun was shining in through the window the next morning when a soft knock sounded on the door.

Gracie opened blurry eyes and yawned, sending one arm into the air.

"Come in?" Then she turned. "Miri—wake up—"

She halted. Miri was not there.

Ellie's voice came from the door. "She went in with Mollie early this morning. Miss Hazel sent me up. She said you need to eat something if you plan on working at the hospital today."

"*Grief!*" Gracie launched herself out of bed toward the wash basin. "Thank you, Ellie."

It was an hour later when she plowed into the dormitory and stalked up behind Miri, who was changing a bandage on the soldier in the bed next to the captain.

"Miri Clarke! You are such a pain in the ass—" she paused abruptly, as she glanced behind Miri and saw the expression on the captain's face. "*Sorry*. Why didn't you tell me you were leaving early? You scared me to death!"

Miri turned to face her and put both hands on her hips. Her voice was not much softer than Gracie's. "Because you were asleep, you dolt. I figured after keeping you up half the night talking, you needed to rest."

"After having a nightmare and waking half the *house,* you mean?"

"*Gracie.*" Miri's arms dropped to her sides.

Gracie looked past her to see the scowling captain in the next bed, and then back at Miri. "Well, if you ever do that again, I'll be furious. I was worried about you." She turned and flounced toward the front of the building to put on an apron.

MIRI WAS MUTTERING UNDER HER BREATH. "I swear. No one *ever* wonders what's on Gracie's mind." She sighed and turned back to the young soldier whose bandage she had begun changing. A few moments later it was finished.

The patient was chuckling now. "What a pleasant start to the day."

"Gracie is a dear." She smiled back at him. "But there seems to be no guard between her brain and her mouth." Her hand flew to her mouth suddenly. "Oh! I really shouldn't have said that, either. My apologies, sir."

"Quite all right. I thought for a moment you were sisters."

Miri only smiled. "Is this better? We're finished."

"Perfect, miss. You're very good at this."

"Thank you." Miri was about to ask if she could bring him anything, when she glanced over and saw Nate crooking his finger at her.

He was not smiling.

"Come here, young lady," his deep voice sounded completely serious.

"I... need to wash my hands first, Captain."

"Nate."

She nodded, and took up the old bandages, putting them in a container, before going into the bath to wash her hands for the twentieth time that morning. When she came out Nate's eyes followed her all the way across the room to his bed.

He reached out and took hold of her arm as soon as she was near enough. Pulling her closer, he lifted her chin with his left hand.

"What's this about a nightmare?" When he felt her stiffen, he added, "Answer me, young lady."

Her glance darted around the room furtively. "Nate, I cannot—"

Tears were gathering; she knew he saw them, and he pulled her to him, wrapping an arm around her. "Shh, Miri. I know I don't have the right to demand that you tell me, but I want to know. And when I'm alone with you, I shall expect it. Understand?"

She raised her gaze to his and tried to leave his embrace, shocked at his demand. But instead he tightened his grip. Catching Gracie's eye from where she stood, he motioned her toward them.

Her eyes widened, but she came. She stopped at the end of the bed, however, and would not come closer.

"Just a warning," he ordered, looking from one to the other. "If you two girls decide to argue again, you will do it outside. Is that clear? The other soldiers can do without the amusement."

Gracie nodded as her eyes filled with new respect, and she backed away with a "Yes, sir." She took a deep breath and returned to her work. Miri moved to do the same, but he kept her in his grasp.

"Miri? Do you understand me?" His voice was slightly gruff.

"Yes, sir." She looked up and nodded.

He continued to stare down at her. "I realize you didn't start the argument. But you could have refrained from name-calling."

Her mouth fell open slightly; her expression incredulous. A moment later, she closed it again.

"If you have a problem," he added, "you can come to me."

Miri stared back at him in disbelief. There had

been no hesitation in his voice at all. It was as if expecting her to come to him was quite natural.

"You cannot be serious, Nate." She gave a slight shake of her head.

His stare became a scowl. "You look surprised. I'm entirely serious. If you have a problem you may come to me. If it's at all possible, I shall take care of it. Understood?"

"All right." It came out as a whisper, but the disbelief was in it was evident.

He pulled her closer until her face was a foot from his. "And in the meantime, there will be no arguments between you and Gracie in this room in front of the soldiers. Is that clear?"

She blinked, and her gaze fell. "Yes... sir."

He ran the back of his hand gently along her cheek. "And now that I have scolded you yet again, I shall let you return to your work." He released her, and she hastened quickly out of his reach. But when she reached the end of his bed, she turned back, scowling.

"Has anyone changed your bandage today, sir?"

"No."

"I see."

Miri went to the bath to pick up the clean cloths, however she waited quite a long time before returning with them.

"I didn't think you were coming back. Does it frighten you to be near me?"

She looked up, troubling her lower lip with her teeth.

"If it does, it's because you're quite... iron-handed, Captain Alley."

He smiled. "Iron-handed. Indeed? And what happened to '*Nate?*'"

"I shall use it again when you become less tyrannical."

"Hm." The captain leaned back against the headboard and watched as she deftly removed the soiled cloths that covered his chest. He said nothing until she had finished, but when the last clean bandage was in place, he took hold of her wrist.

"Before you go," he said gently, "I need to ask you a question."

She raised her eyes to his.

"The Doctor thinks I may possibly go home tomorrow and finish recovering in your care. But before I do, I want to speak with you privately. When I sit up this afternoon, I want to see you in the kitchen alone. Is that agreeable?"

She stared at him. "I... suppose so."

"Good. Because I have some questions for you. And I want to set some rules."

"Rules?" Her voice rose.

"Your eyes have paled into a very light shade of blue, Miri. You heard me. These are rules that apply to us; you and me," he breathed. "Go now if you need. But be thinking about it. We'll discuss it further this afternoon."

All Miri could do was to nod when he let her move away.

Rules? What sort of rules? She was frowning as she took the soiled cloths to their container.

What could he possibly mean by this?

She was coming out of the bath after washing her hands, when familiar arms clasped her around the neck. It was Gracie.

"I'm so sorry, Miri, and I apologize. I was wrong when I fussed at you this morning. After last night's dream, I was worried when I awakened this morning and found you gone." She looked apologetic. "I let my temper get the better of me."

"And I apologize for calling you a dolt." Miri's voice was just a whisper, but when Gracie smiled and hugged her back, cheers went up around the room. The soldiers were watching, after all.

"Oh dear," Gracie made a face. "Your captain was right, after all. William would have been quite upset with me if he'd been here."

Miri only grinned. "Well, *I* won't tell him. Your secret is safe with me."

They both returned to their work, but Miri found herself pondering Nate's words. *Tomorrow*, he'd said. If she were to care for him, would she not be working here after that? Dr. Foster had not said a word to her this morning about Nate's release.

If you have a problem, you may come to me.

Miri thought about those words with longing. How long had it been since she had someone to go to? Since Burton's death, certainly. She felt her roles had changed in the past few years. She had become the person others seemed to come to with their problems. Could Nate possibly mean what he said?

Her shoulders relaxed. It would be wonderful to have his strong and secure arms to lean on. Without realizing it, she looked over at his bed. He was leaning back with his eyes closed, a peaceful expression on his handsome face. She waited for him to move, desperate for the assurance he was all right.

He didn't.

She became rigid as she waited. Her breath caught in her throat, and suddenly she flew toward his bed.

Just then, Nate moved his hand and opened his eyes, resting them upon Miri. Abruptly she stopped and turned away, trying not to show the relief she felt at the reassurance he was all right.

He was studying her now, concern on his face. "Miri?"

Forcing a nod, she turned and disappeared into the kitchen.

He's all right, Miri. She closed her eyes, her breath coming in great gasps. *But what if...*

"No. *No.* I can't do this."

It hit her as she realized it. She'd almost gone to pieces in the space of only a few seconds as she thought she'd lost him, too.

Four years ago, she'd promised Burton over his gravesite she would never allow herself to love another. It was a promise she was sure she could keep. Now, as she leaned back against the wall with her hand balled into a fist and clasped over her heart, she suddenly felt as if she'd betrayed him.

She moved to the window and stared outside at the snow, showing brilliant crystals as it glittered in the sun.

For a brief moment, she there once again, standing by Burton's grave. She could see his face smiling down at her.

Dear, *dear* Burton.

8

Confession...

"Miri?" Gracie opened the door and looked in. "There you are. Mrs. Thatcher is coming across with a pot of something. She may need help. I'm right outside the door, but I'm in the middle of changing a bandage."

Miri nodded. "I'll check and see," she said, following Gracie out into the room.

The captain's gaze was resting on her now, his brow raised and his expression curious. She looked instantly away and blinked.

Before she reached the parlor, Marilyn Thatcher entered, carrying an enormous pot of stew.

"May I help you, Mrs. Thatcher?"

"Yes, Miri. There is more in the church kitchen, if you can help me bring it across. The soldiers there have eaten, but they were hungry little fellows today. Natalie and I ended up having to throw together another two pots."

Gracie followed Miri into the kitchen with Jennifer behind her. "I'm finished now. We can begin to ladle it into some bowls and pass them out," she offered.

"Thank you, Gracie. I hope there's enough for all the soldiers here, but I fear there won't be. Miri and I shall return with the rest."

As Miri followed Marilyn toward the door, she glanced toward the captain and smiled. He winked back at her.

Marilyn turned toward her as soon as they exited the front door. "Am I losing my mind, or did that handsome young soldier just wink at you?"

Miri grinned, and Marilyn began to laugh. "I thought so! Miri Clarke, I know I've always said handsome is as handsome does, but judging by the color in your cheeks, you must think this one is very nice."

Miri glanced across the street toward the church, looking for a way to change the topic. "So, um, what did you end up with in the other two pots?"

Marilyn laughed. "I hope they can't tell it's a conglomeration of spare parts. We did borrow some of Father Michael's stew," She said, leaning forward, "and added a bit of chicken to it. And some other things."

Miri laughed. "What other things?"

"Hm, another story for another day. Natalie and I both told him this was our confession for the week and he was bound to silence. And do you know?" She gave off a girlish giggle. "He had the nerve to say it doesn't work that way?"

Miri hooted with laughter. "Poor Father Michael. But I'm still curious. What *did* you put in it?"

"Hm. A little of this, a little of that. And a lot of salt and pepper and spices. And I don't remember what else. Oh my, I do hope you brought another batch of cookies today for the soldiers in the dormitory, because the ones in the hall ate all those we had, too."

Miri found herself trying to contain her mirth as she opened the door into the church hall. It was quite easy to see where Merrie inherited her bubbly nature.

As they entered the hall, Merriweather's innocent voice reached them. She was reading *Pride and Prejudice* to the soldiers, imitating the voice of Mrs. Bennett. The soldiers were holding blankets and pillows to their wounds to keep the jarring from their laughter to a minimum.

Miri entered the kitchen, where Father Michael was eyeing the pots on the stove with suspicion.

"Hello, Father," she said, moving toward him to stand in front of the pots. She took a whiff. Both of them contained something that resembled chicken stew with beef.

"Hello, my child."

Miri glanced at him curiously. He had raised a brow, and finally picked up a spoon and sampled the contents.

"Well," he said thoughtfully, "I don't suppose it will hurt them."

"What is it?" Miri whispered.

"It's..." he paused, "something akin to chicken and dumplings. But without the dumplings... and only a little chicken... and some beef, and... other things." He finished as Marilyn entered, and he winked at Miri.

Miri grinned. "I'll just say it's a secret recipe."

By the time they crossed to the staircase once again, Merrie was portraying the voice of Mr. Collins, the stuffy visiting vicar who was intent on proposing to Miss Elizabeth Bennett. The soldiers in the room were laughing hysterically, and Miri looked back at Mrs. Thatcher, who was rolling her eyes and shaking her head.

"My daughter has the best job of all of us," she said, as she made sure the street outside was clear enough to cross.

"And, I think," Miri replied, "the one that is the most healing."

∘✦∘

MOLLIE WAS WAITING IMPATIENTLY BY THE TIME she arrived, and eagerly began spooning the soup from the new pot into bowls to deliver. Gracie was washing up the bowls as quickly as possible to reuse.

Miri glanced at the clock above the hearth as her hand slid into her pocket. She had not yet delivered the supply order to the General Store, and a few moments later she left to take it across the street. The captain watched her go back toward the door with her basket and frowned as she waved. She couldn't help but notice the frown on his face. But she couldn't wait long enough to explain to him what she was doing. That would have to be explained later.

She paused long enough to kick the mud off her boots before going inside. Natalie Greene was arranging things and turned to face her.

"It's so good to see you, Miri. I have the kettle on. Come back and have a cup of tea with me? You're the first person I have seen all day who didn't have a blue uniform or an apron on."

"I would dearly love that, Miss Natalie. And how

are you, Mr. Greene?" She handed him the supply list. He smiled when he saw it.

"This is quite a list," he said, raising a brow.

"Yes sir. Benjamin will be in later to pick it up." She leaned forward, murmuring. "Would it be all right if he loads from the back, sir?"

"Certainly, Miri. I'll figure up the totals while you relax for a moment. Natalie has been cooking all morning with Marilyn Thatcher, and she's ready for a rest. All the ladies in town seem to be working at the hospitals."

But Mrs. Greene had put her head back in. "Come, child. You work yourself to death. You need to take a moment and rest."

Miri smiled and followed as Natalie closed the door between the store and the back room. Through that, she led Miri toward her kitchen and closed the door, motioning her toward the table.

"Sit, Miri. Your eyes tell me you're exhausted."

"Thank you, ma'am. I must admit, I am tired."

Pulling out a set of China cups and saucers, Natalie leaned forward. "I have something to tell you. And actually, I something I wish to ask."

Miri looked up. "Yes, ma'am?"

"I heard the Confederates have taken over Merrie's house."

Miri stared at her, unsure how much information she should give away. But the kettle was whistling on the stove now, and Natalie reached for it to pour, shaking her head. "Marilyn told me about it. What I want to know is how we can help. She said Merrie and Katie and the staff all went to Pembroke. And she also said Ellie's house was taken by the Union. I knew about Gracie's, but not Ellie's."

Miri sighed. "It's true, Miss Natalie. All of it."

"That makes a tremendous amount of people to be fed at Pembroke. But Miri, you all need to keep their presence quiet. I certainly won't tell anyone. What I want to know is if my husband and I may help in any way at all. I know times are tough for everyone now, but Mr. Greene and I would like to help with the costs of supplies."

Miri was impressed. "May I send Angel over to speak with you? I know she would be very appreciative of your offer. You're so sweet, but I already know how much you do for the hospitals, ma'am."

Natalie waved her comment away. "Nonsense. This is our home. Everyone is suffering during these dreadful times. Now, tell me what is happening with the ladies and children there."

Miri shared as much as she dared; it was good to relax for a moment, but when she looked up at the clock, she realized how late it was. The captain might be anxious by now; after all, he'd wished to speak with her this afternoon.

Giving Natalie a hug and a sincere word of thanks, she moved through the back room and opened the door to the store. As she paid Mr. Greene, she noticed the total for the bill was not as high as she expected. Giving him a hug and a word of thanks, she left.

So, the Greenes knew the people from the Adams House had vacated the estate and sought refuge at Pembroke. Miri knew they could be trusted to keep it quiet. Yet a thought lingered in the back of her mind.

Who else knew besides the Greenes? And worse, how long would it be before Pembroke was robbed of their supplies?

She heard a shout, and stepped up her pace across the muddy street, lifting the skirts of her gown to keep them dry. Kicking off the as much mud as possible from her boots outside the door, she opened it and went inside. She was unsure what time Captain Alley had wanted to see her, but she had indeed been gone a long time.

The first thing Mollie said to her as she tightened the apron about her waist made her smile.

"The soldiers are raving about today's soup, Miri. And some of them asked for another bowl. Please tell

Mrs. Thatcher and Father Michael they would like it made as often as possible."

Miri stared as she watched Mollie retreat. In the back of her mind she could hear Marilyn's words when she'd asked what was in it.

"Oh, a little of this, a little of that..."

She moved into the empty kitchen just in time to cover her mouth to hide her laughter.

9

A *discussion...*

MIRI SCANNED THE LARGE ROOM AS SHE ENTERED, and gasped. The captain was standing up next to the bed, looking worried, toward the door. Dr. Foster was trying to get him to sit back down on his bed, but he was not complying.

She rushed toward him. Ignoring Dr. Foster, he looked down at her.

"*Where* have you been, young lady? I was worried."

Miri's face took on a deep scowl. "There was something important I had to do this afternoon, Captain."

"You could have explained that. Are you quite ready to speak with me?"

"Yes."

"In the kitchen. Now," he said, in the voice she was extremely familiar with by this time. "Dr. Foster, would you mind helping me?"

Doctor Foster seemed to realize Nate was not about to sit back down. He moved to one side while Miri stayed on the other; each of them reached around him with one arm in case he became weak. Slowly, they made it to the kitchen with him.

Nate glanced around the room and lowered himself down onto the bench, facing away from the table. Miri was surprised at how strong his gait was.

Dr. Foster turned to Miri as soon as Nate sat down. He looked as if he had quite reached the end of his patience.

"*Don't dare* to let him try to get back to bed on his own. I do plan to release him—possibly tomorrow. And Miri, as much as we need you here, I want you to stay home with this man and care for him until he's completely well. Having the two of you here in the same room—and Gracie on top of that, is giving me a headache. The soldiers are quite entertained by it, but I'm too old for this kind of nonsense in my hospital. Understand? You may come back when

Captain Alley is well and can be trusted to behave himself at home alone."

Miri's gaze fell as she hung her head wearily. "I understand, sir."

Dr. Foster left the room, and Miri raised her head angrily, staring at Nate. "Thank you, Captain, for getting me fired from my responsibilities."

His only response was to point back toward the main room. "Bring in the stool sitting beside my bed."

She glared at him. Exiting the kitchen, she brought the stool and carried it through the door. He reached out a hand toward it, and she held it out toward him.

Nate took it and set it down right in front of him. He pointed.

"Sit."

She continued to stare. "Do you think me a dog, sir?"

His brows rose.

"Miri Clarke, if I have to pick you up and put you there, I will."

Her gaze remained on his face, her mouth flat. Finally, she sighed and sat down. Nate nodded and took hold of the little stool, edging it closer. He leaned forward until his face was only inches from hers.

"I want you to tell me as much as you can about the arrangements at Pembroke."

His request surprised her. "I can tell you what I know. Miss Hazel has not yet shared all of them with me. I only know she's preparing a room for you on the ground floor close to the front door. There will be staff from the Adams house nearby if you should need anything in the middle of the night. Miss Mollie will be close by as well, so if you need a nurse we shall both be there to help."

His scowl deepened. "And where will you be?"

She looked somewhat taken aback. "I don't yet know for certain."

"Don't make assumptions, young lady. Just answer my question. Where do you normally sleep?"

"On the third floor, with the other ladies. We— Gracie and I share a room."

He cocked his head. "And you don't kill each other?"

She laughed. "No. We get along quite well most of the time."

"Well, that's good news. I'm glad you're so far up. You should be safer at night."

He was staring down at her, but she wasn't sure exactly where his thoughts were. Finally, he spoke once again.

"Another question. How many firearms do you

have in the house? Do you know how to shoot? Any of you? Can you protect yourselves? Can *you* handle a rifle or a shotgun without it knocking you flat on your back?"

Miri glanced toward the door. "I'd rather not discuss it here, sir. But I'll be happy to tell you tomorrow on the way home, where it's more private?"

He searched her face. "That makes sense. I'm getting ahead of myself."

She met his eyes. He was nodding and she could tell he was deep in thought. "The conversation you overheard yesterday between the Major and me was regarding a request that he would order the Cavalry to leave Pembroke alone."

"I did hear him say that."

"I thought you might. Then you likely heard him say he couldn't promise they would follow orders. All right. My next question is, do you have enough food there to take care of a houseful of staff, plus all the ones who moved in? And another soldier?"

"You mean you, sir. Yes. We've worked out a plan. But again, I'd rather wait to discuss it until we're in a place where no one will overhear. I promise to tell you as soon as we're on our way home."

He frowned and nodded. "You're a wise girl."

"Thank you."

They sat there, staring into each other's eyes, for

a long moment. Finally, Nate put his hands on her shoulders. "It occurs to me a good many of the questions I have will have to wait, then. So now we come to the part we must discuss. The part about you. And about me."

"What... about you—a-and me—Captain?"

His mouth turned up slightly. "Do you only have that adorable little stutter when you're unsure what to say?"

She blinked at him. "Is," she took a deep breath, rehearsing, and started again. "Is it obvious?"

"No. Only when you think I might be a bit perturbed with you, as far as I can see."

She lowered her head until she found herself staring at his chest and then tried to look away once again. "When Angel—Lady Angel—and I came out here, I stuttered badly. But when Burton and I married, he worked with me for several years to help me overcome it. It still bothers me sometimes—at the most—" she took a breath, "*inappropriate* times. But it's so much better now. And Burton..." she paused.

He cocked his head. "Yes?"

"He encouraged me to learn to read and write. Miss Ellie was teaching Saturday classes and he attended them. After we married, we both went together. My mother never thought school was important for girls. But Burton was such an encourager."

When she looked up, he was smiling. "Indeed, it seems so."

She was quiet, waiting until he spoke again, and having no idea what she should say.

"Miri, I wish to tell you a bit about myself." He took a deep breath. "I'm sure you realize I'm not always the most patient of men. Don't laugh; I know how obvious it is. Sometimes I speak before considering my words carefully enough. You've seen that already. But I'm quick to apologize when I know I'm wrong. And I do try my best to look out for those who are my responsibility." He stopped and rolled his eyes. "I'm doing a wretched job of this, aren't I?" He lifted her chin, his eyes narrowed down at her. "Please listen carefully."

She kept her gaze upward, waiting.

"I told you this morning if you had any problems, you were free to come to me. Do you understand what I meant by it?"

Miri shook her head slowly. "No, sir."

"Well, damnation," he said, frustrated. "I'm totally inadequate at this. I think Dr. Foster must have removed part of my brain."

A laugh bubbled out from her.

"And another thing you should know. I spank little girls who laugh at me."

Her smile disappeared, and she tried to back away from his hand, but his hold on her chin deepened. "What I mean is this. I've been watching you every minute since the very first morning I awakened to find you hovering over me with your invisible angel's wings. I could feel them fanning me with concern. You fascinate me, Miri. I know I haven't been patient with you, and I have scolded you and threatened you on far too many occasions. But the truth? I've come to care about you deeply. How can I say this?" He took both her hands into his. "It would make me extremely proud if you would consider being *mine*."

Miri's mouth dropped open slightly. "Y-yours?"

"Yes. Mine. I'm not asking you to marry me—*yet*. I'd like to give you time to get to know me. You may run away screaming when you finally do. But I want you to know whether you can put up with all my faults before I ask. But you must know, Miri, I'm incredibly drawn to you. You're beautiful. You're capable. You take everyone's needs very seriously. You're a nurturer by nature. But it's more than that."

She was continuing to stare blankly at him, and he squeezed her hands.

"There is a connection we have. And it is my desire to take care of you."

"I... don't know what to say, Captain—"

He smiled. "Once again, my girl. Nate."

"Nate."

"But I do expect you to know I'm accustomed to expecting strict obedience. And I shall indeed expect it from you."

She had looked away, and he brought her face back to his, tenderly drawing the back of his fingers along her cheek. "Now," he breathed softly, leaning forward to kiss her forehead. "You have not answered my question, which is... would you consider being mine?"

Miri cherished the words as they fell from his tongue. She remembered the nightmare from last night, and the sheer terror she felt as she had dreamt the dead man was Nate. She continued to stare as she ran her tongue along her lower lip to moisten it. "Yes, sir. I believe I would like that," she whispered, "very much."

Nate placed his hands on both sides of her face and lifted it to his just before he leaned down further to plant a kiss on her mouth.

MIRI LISTENED TO THE OTHERS CHATTER ABOUT their day on the way home, but her mind was elsewhere. She thought of his kiss all the way home as she stared out the window. No one else seemed to notice.

Before she had risen to her feet to go for Dr. Foster, Nate had pulled her back down onto the stool in front of him. With his right hand he wrapped her hair around his fist, gently tilting her head back. Once again he leaned forward, kissing her forehead, then the tip of her nose, and then her mouth as her heart pounded.

When Nate raised his head, his dark glittering eyes held hers.

"*Go.*"

Miri could feel her heart even now, pounding fiercely in her chest. That same jolt of electricity occurred and she trembled, just thinking of his mouth on hers.

❧ 10 ☙

C *hanging places...*

MIRI CONTINUED THE RIDE HOME IN SILENCE. THE
ladies had chattered until they passed Merrie's, and
then Angel turned toward her.

"How was your day with the captain today, Miri?"

Gracie groaned. "I think between us, we got her
fired."

"What!" Ellie sounded appalled. "What
happened?"

Merrie's eyes were enormous, and Angel gasped in
disbelief.

"I... well.." Gracie looked from one to another

with a remorseful expression. "I think I caused it to begin with. And then the captain scolded us both for arguing in front of the soldiers. He said we were never to do that again."

Miri nodded. "Dr. Foster came in this afternoon and told me to stay home and nurse Nate back to health. He plans on releasing him tomorrow. He said between the three of us, we gave him headaches."

"But you're the best nurse he has! Oh—sorry Gracie," Merrie shook her head. "I didn't mean—"

"No, it's true and we all know it," Gracie said in a tone of lament. "But at least this way, Miri gets to spend time with her captain. And," she said, grinning with mischief, "he really is *her* captain now."

"Gracie!" Miri admonished, her eyes wide.

"Well, it's true. They might as well know. I think Dr. Foster did that on purpose. Of course, *I* shall have to work twice as hard, but I don't mind. I have to stay busy to keep from being so... morose." She looked out the window and Miri leaned over and hugged her.

A moment later, Merrie turned to her. "Is this true, Miri? About you and the captain?"

Miri hesitated. It was difficult to put their relationship into words. "Nate says that he wishes to look out for me, but how can I be sure what to expect?" She looked back out the window and sighed, determined not to share his actual words with them.

Gracie nodded vigorously. "Well, I for one don't envy you, Miri. As for me, I'd hate to try to care for him as a patient, even though he *is* a gorgeous bit of soldier. But..."

"Gracie!" Merrie's eyes were round and surprised. "You'd better be glad we're all your dearest friends. If we weren't, we might just tell William what you just said!"

"But I was *going* to say," Gracie's expression was firm, "I would much rather have my William back. And he's gorgeous, too."

The carriage began to slow, and they looked up to see the lights of Pembroke.

Miri was the last one to descend from the coach. She watched with amusement as a herd of children surrounded them all just inside the entryway. Cissy and Polly swarmed around their mother while Thomas bowed in the background. This evening, however, the twins seemed to be pouting.

"Mama! You should have been here to protect us!" Cissy's lower lip protruded as she spoke.

Ellie's face paled. "From what? What happened?"

"It's Abel." Polly frowned, her beautiful chestnut curls bouncing. "He's so mean!"

"Ah," a suspicious note crept into Ellie's voice as

she glanced with mirth at Miri. Ellie studied both her daughters curiously. "But you forget how well I know you, my darlings. And what makes you say Abel is mean, Mary Polly?"

"He is, Mama!" Cissy, her sister's twin in every detail, chimed in. "He says we're poorly behaved, and we should be taken to the—umm."

"To the woodshed." Polly finished triumphantly. "Able is *very* mean."

Ellie put her hands on her hips as she eyed the miniatures of herself with skepticism. "And just what were you two doing before he said that?" She paused at their hesitation. "Girls?"

"Um," the twins looked at each other. Obviously, they had not thought their argument through.

Thomas merely nodded to his mother from where he stood. "*Abel is quite right, Mother*."

Miss Betsy came downstairs, just then. "I'm so glad you have them, Ellie. Emily has been chasing them all over the house. Geoffrey Francis and Nicholas and Thomas have been trying to find them. Abel, too, but I think he has taught them how to hide a little too well."

Angel grinned. "I hope it has not upset Miss Hazel too much."

Miss Betsy rolled her eyes. "You jest, Lady Angel.

Miss Hazel dotes on them. She lets them get away with anything their little hearts desire."

Angel's laugh rang through the house as Mrs. Betsy and Ellie herded the girls back up to the third-floor nursery.

But Merrie paused as she caught a glimpse of Abel standing a few feet away. She knew Miss Hazel was right; Abel, although not as tall as the *Sentinels*, had certainly grown.

"*Abel!*" she whispered, "How are you?"

"I'm well, Lady Adams." He bowed politely, first to Merrie, then to Miri as she smiled and waved at him. His tousled hair was the same shade of dark brown as was his father's. But he had Kathleen's blue eyes, and they were flashing now.

"What I said to Cissy and Polly is the truth. They were hiding today and climbed inside the buffet in the dining room where all the dishes are kept. When they climbed back out, they dragged out some of the china onto the floor with them and broke it. And the blue crystal lamp Lady Angel loves so much that was on top? Cissy reached up and pulled on the doily where it sits. Miss Hazel was close by, and she caught the lamp just before it hit the floor."

Merrie gasped. "Oh, Abel! Thank goodness it was spared. Perhaps I should encourage Angel to pack it away. Is that why the twins think you're mean?

Because they're worried Angel will find out about the lamp and the dishes?"

Abel shook his head. "No, ma'am, that's not it. They've been trading places all day during our schooling. Cissy hates numbers, but loves history, and Polly loves numbers but hates history, so they change places during those classes, and Miss Emily doesn't even know. I threatened to tell her. That's why they think I'm mean."

Merrie straightened up. "But *you* can tell them apart? I can't."

He nodded. "Yes, ma'am. Perhaps Mrs. Andrews should dress them differently, instead of always alike. Changing places and fooling people is their favorite game."

"Ahh. I see. Abel?" A wide smile spread across Merrie's face. "Has anyone told you just how *brilliant* you are?"

He smiled and bowed once more, saying, "No, Lady Adams. Not brilliant. Just observant."

છ‍ે‍ક

THE CAPTAIN'S QUARTERS...

Miss Hazel drew Miri into the room prepared for Nate and showed her how it was arranged.

"I hope this is satisfactory, Miss Miri," she

explained. "You should be comfortable enough during the day while you care for him. And the maid's room can be used during the night for a week or so, until the captain is able to get around well enough on his own."

Miri nodded gratefully. "Thank you, Miss Hazel. I believe I shall have everything I need here for his care. He will be released tomorrow, if everything goes as planned."

Miss Hazel nodded thoughtfully. "And Miss Constance and I should like you three ladies to meet with us in the library after supper to see if you have made final plans?"

"Yes ma'am. It is put into motion. It started today with me, but I'll give you a copy of the schedule this evening."

"Good. I'm eager to see it."

It took only a few moments. She told them about her conversation with Mrs. Greene, and their offer to help.

"The Greenes know we're full here, and need a lot of supplies. I explained Angel will come and speak with her. But when I paid the bill—it already seemed to me they had not charged us full price."

"You're quite right. Benjamin brought it to me. I will go over it with Lady Angel," she said, nodding.

"Thank you, Miri. I always know I may count on you."

THE NIGHT PASSED FITFULLY FOR MIRI. GRACIE tossed and turned and talked in her sleep, and Miri awakened frequently.

Her own dreams were troubled as well. She pulled out the last of Burton's posts just before climbing into bed, and read it by the lamplight. Padding to the window, she stood there a long time, looking out at the moonlit snow with Burton's post clasped tightly in her hands. The moon was bright tonight, and the moon gave the snow around Burton's grave a glow.

"Come to bed, my friend. You need to sleep." Gracie's gentle voice interrupted her thoughts.

Miri nodded and climbed back into bed, failing to realize she still held Burton's parchment tightly in her hand.

Over and over again, in her dreams, she read it word for word. She knew it was because she'd memorized every word over the past few years.

At the end of it, however, there was a disturbing change. Something wasn't right, and she brought the parchment closer to her face, holding it up before the firelight to see.

She gasped, suddenly.

Instead of being signed with Burton's name, the signature now read,

"Your devoted and loving husband,
Nate."

GOING HOME...

WHEN THE SUN CAME IN THROUGH THE WINDOWS the next morning, she was still quite disturbed. She wondered if Nate's sleep had been any less disrupted.

The first thing she did when she awakened was to look for Burton's post. Somehow, she knew she'd taken it to bed with her last night.

When she turned, Gracie's eyes were resting on her as she yawned and stretched.

"What are you looking for, my friend?"

Without answering, Miri kept searching.

Gracie sat up in bed. "This?" She asked, holding out her hand.

Miri stared at her. In the hand Gracie extended

was the last post Burton had sent. She eagerly reached for it.

"When I awakened last night, you were crumpling it to death," Gracie grinned. "Sad way for a love letter from a husband to go. Here."

Miri grabbed it hurriedly and found the last page. The signature at the end now bore Burton's name, in his own script. Miri put a relieved hand to her chest.

A frown crossed Gracie's face. "What is it?"

Miri glanced away, closing her eyes. "Nothing."

The sympathy in Gracie's face touched her, and Miri finally rested a hand on her shoulder. "Thank you for caring, dear Gracie."

When Miri came through the door into the dormitory, Nate was dressed in his uniform and was sitting in the chair next to the bed.

Miri walked quietly over to him and put her hands on her hips.

"It will be a long ride to Pembroke, Captain. You'd be wise to stay in bed until we're ready to leave."

"I'm ready." He said, attempting to rise from the chair.

Miri pushed him back down gently. "We're going

nowhere until I can discuss your care with Dr. Foster. Please, *sit*."

"Enough, sassylass. I'm ready to leave, and I've had quite enough of this bed. Make it fast."

She sighed and rolled her eyes as she went to locate the doctor. He was in the kitchen discussing the care of his patients with Mollie.

"Ah, Miri, there you are," he said. "It's a relief to see you. I'm more than ready for you to take your patient home and get him out of my hospital ward before he rips open an incision. I swear, I've even had nightmares about him falling to pieces and leaving body parts scattered across my hospital."

Miri's grin reached her eyes. "So have I, sir. I just came in to see what your guidelines are for his care."

"Check his wound when he gets home. And again tomorrow. After that, you can do it every other day, unless he appears to be bleeding. He can eat anything he wants now. And he can have laudanum for pain, but as it is he's refusing it. Watch for fever, and monitor for signs of infection. Come or send someone for me if you need anything. That's all. And," he chuckled, grinning, "if you're able to put up with his recalcitrance, you will have done better than I."

She groaned. "I shall do my best, sir."

Mollie nodded. "I'll check in on him every day or

so, Miri. But if you need me, call. I'll be sleeping in the house."

"Thank you, Miss Mollie."

Miri approached Nate with a wide grin. But as she grew closer, he pulled himself up to stand.

"Captain Alley!" she barked, realizing she sounded very much like Mollie. "If you cannot wait long enough for me to find someone to help you to the carriage, I shall refuse to take you home."

His face etched with lines as she watched, and his eyes narrowed. There was well over a foot of height difference, yet Miri put both hands on her hips and glared back up at him; her tiny 5' to his 6' 4" frame. Dr. Foster corralled him on one side; Mollie and Miri on the other, until he nodded.

"*Sassylass*," he muttered under his breath.

THE TRIP TO PEMBROKE WAS SLOW. BENJAMIN HAD paused outside the dormitory as the Major stopped by to bring Nate's remaining belongings to him. It was comprised of his footlocker and papers, his extra uniform and a few other supplies he'd left behind when he was injured. Nate was already inside the carriage when the Major put his head in.

"Wear your uniform, Captain. I don't care if

you're legally discharged. Keep the appearance of still being a Union Soldier. You may have less trouble that way from the group of soldiers still hanging about. And keep your rifle handy, but don't dare use it yet." He paused to smile at Miri. "And you have my permission to make him behave."

Miri stared at him in surprise. "That, sir, is an impossibility," she said simply.

The Major threw back his head and laughed. "Missy, I can tell you this. He does what he wants. That's not always popular in the Army chain of command. But I have yet to see an instance where Captain Alley made the wrong decision. Ever." He nodded toward Nate and saluted before closing the door behind him.

Miri and Nate sat facing each other. His face still held a scowl.

"You, young lady," he said, his face chiseled, "are in trouble as soon as I have my strength back. You may depend upon it."

She sighed. "I hope I haven't agreed to more than I can handle."

"You'd prefer I lay down and die?"

"No!" It was a shout; then suddenly she shook her head. "No," she said, again, "I would not. Please don't speak that way—"

Surprised at her outburst, he reached across and drew the back of his hand down her cheek.

"Miri?"

She leaned forward and reached up one hand to touch his cheek."Please, Nate.." she whispered, "Please *don't ever say that again*."

He caught her wrist and brought her palm to his lips. Very gently he kissed it.

"I promise, Miri. I shall not."

T o Pembroke...

THE TRIP HOME WAS NOT AS STILTED AND JERKY AS she'd feared. She saw him wince a time or two, but he didn't complain. His hands held hers across the seat as she faced him.

Miri watched. His position was rigid during the ride, and she could tell he was relieved when the carriage pulled up in the back of the house. They had witnessed a few of the Cavalry in the area, but not as many as Miri had seen in the past few days.

"I asked Benjamin to bring us to the back so there would be no steps to climb. Please stay," Miri beseeched, putting up a hand, "until we can get someone to help get you inside?"

"Perhaps you should get someone a bit more substantial than you," he said.

Her expression was concerned. It was his first concession that he felt weak. Benjamin and Sebastian, however, appeared at the door, and flanked him on each side as soon as they got him to the ground. Miri followed, along with both Miss Hazel and Miss Constance.

A moment later, he was in the blue room in the front of the house, and lying down on the bed. His eyes closed, and his face took on a look of pallor.

Miri felt for his pulse and then leaned her head down on his upper chest, listening for the beat of his heart.

Miss Hazel leaned forward. "Is he all right?"

"He sounds steady and strong," Miri whispered, turning to look up at her.

Nate opened his eyes and scowled. "I'm fine. And my hearing works well too, so enough of speaking of me as if I'm not here."

Miri sighed softly and glanced at the housekeepers. Miss Constance had a brow raised; Miss Hazel's eyes crinkled at the corners. Sebastian and Benjamin exchanged glances of amusement.

Nate looked around the room, eyeing everyone who stood there.

Mrs. Hazel spoke first. "Captain? Is there anything we can get you? Is the room comfortable? We shall bring some fresh water. Would you like something to eat?"

At that, his eyes lit up. "I would love some water. And yes, a small bit of food too, but please don't go to a great deal of trouble. And the bed is heavenly. Remember, I've slept on the ground for the past five years." His gaze rested on Sebastian and then Benjamin. "Gentlemen, I doubt I could have made it in without your help. Thank you."

Miss Hazel nodded and left. "We shall return. Miri will be in here caring for you. She can stay in the next room at night, in case you need anything."

Miri expected him to argue. But he only smiled, his gaze coming to rest on her. "I shall be fine. Thank you, ma'am."

Miri took a moment to introduce the people in the room, and one by one, they filed out.

"I suppose," he said, his eyes twinkling with mirth, "I should have waited on lunch. But I didn't eat breakfast this morning, even though it smelled quite good."

"And why not?"

"My own reasons."

Miri searched his face. "Sometimes, Nate, I don't understand you."

"Sometimes I fail to understand myself. Have no worries, my girl. And before you go getting sassy on me, I may or may not allow you to stay down here tonight. Hear me? And don't try to lift the footlocker; have the men shove it under the bed where I can get to it."

She rose and took the rest of his belongings to the wardrobe on the other side of the room. But as she readied to close the door to it, she looked back over her shoulder. "Will you promise to let me bring your things to you when you need them? Or should I leave these on the end of your bed? I'm not at all sure I can trust you to call for me."

"Cheeky little brat."

She grinned, showing her dimples.

"I think your dimples are charming. Why have I not seen them before? Tears I have seen, but not laughter."

"I do laugh sometimes, believe it or not," she assured him, still smiling. "There wasn't much to laugh about the past few days."

His face lost its smile. "Come here, Miri."

She finished closing the wardrobe and moved back over. But the Captain slid over toward the middle, and patted the side of the bed.

"Sit."

"I... cannot, sir."

"Nonsense. I want you close enough so I may touch you if I desire."

Miri looked toward the door, but decided that if anyone came, they would likely knock before entering.

"I just don't wish to appear improper."

"I understand. And I won't put you in that position. But neither do I wish you to wear yourself out getting up and down out of a chair. And I want to get up this afternoon and sit for a while." He pointed to the Queen Anne chair a few feet away. "That chair has to be more comfortable than the one I sat in at the hospital."

She nodded. "But you need to rest first. That's important."

She heard a growl from his belly and clapped a hand to her mouth to keep from giggling.

"Don't you dare to laugh at me, little girl."

"You're hopeless. You starve yourself and then complain if someone is amused by your stomach growling."

A knock sounded on the door, and she went to answer it. "Oh! Bobby, come in."

A young man came in, carrying a tray. "Miss Lillie sent me with some food for Captain Alley." He set it down and helped her to raise Nate up in bed, while she plumped pillows up behind his back.

Nate nodded toward him. "Thank you, Bobby. It smells delicious. Please express my thanks to Miss Lillie."

He grinned. "I shall. Is there anything else you need?" He looked around. "There is coffee and tea on the tray, but I'll bring a pitcher of water. And Miss Miri, Lillie sent you a sweet treat. And I shall bring you both a tray at lunch."

"Thank you, Bobby. I appreciate it."

Nate smiled and said his thanks as well. But he stared after the young man when he left.

Miri watched his expression. "You're thinking he looks big and strong, and capable of fighting in the war."

"Not so. I was thinking there must be a reason he isn't."

Miri set the tray across his lap. "Bobby has hemophilia. One scratch could end his life."

He nodded. "What meets the eye is not always so. One might also look at me and say I should be out fighting."

"No." She shook her head vehemently.

"All right, Sassylass. Sit down here next to me while I eat."

Miri smiled and began lifting the lids from the serving dishes.

His eyes grew wide at the array of foods. "May I just say," he murmured, "I believe I've died and gone to heaven."

"Miss Lillie will be happy to hear it. She's been here many years."

"It sounds as if there should be a story behind that."

She nodded. "A *long* story, sir. Miss Lillie was just one of the employees here who was rescued by Lord Wellington or his father. Pembroke, you see, has a long history of offering refuge to those in need. Even I was rescued by Lady Angel and Lord Geoffrey. It's a house full of open arms. And open hearts."

Nate was staring at her. "Tell me," he said softly, "about your rescue."

"I shall," she grinned as she spoke, "*if* you'll eat while I tell you so your food doesn't get cold? It's a long story, too."

He took a bite, and then eyed her. "All right. Talk to me."

She smiled. "I came from Baltimore," she said softly. "My father left when I was two. According to my mother, he had no desire for the responsibility of a husband-or a father. I cannot even remember what he looked like. So my mother worked hard; she took in laundry, and worked wherever she could, to make enough to feed us. When I grew old enough, I helped with what I could. Laundry, sewing for people. When I turned eighteen, she said she couldn't afford for me to live at home anymore, and began to search for a job for me."

"You were a child," he said, setting down his fork and reaching over to touch her cheek, gently.

"She didn't think so. And she was successful in finding one."

"Doing what?"

"I was to go to Woodstock to work as a lady's maid for a family down there. An old family. They were very proper, and I..." She looked down, shaking her head with embarrassment. "Eat, Nate."

"And you..." He was scowling. "And you *what,* Miri?"

"And I had the terrible stutter then. Their son came to Baltimore to speak with my mother and I, but she arranged it so I wasn't there. She told him I had experience, and he hired me to come, and paid for a ticket so I could ride the stage to Woodstock. But when I came home early, he was still there, and he heard me speak."

A terrible frown etched Nate's face. But his voice, when he spoke, was still gentle. "What happened then?"

"He seemed a very—strange and cruel man, and I begged my mother not to send me. But she said she could no longer afford to feed me. I went to catch the stage and waited outside the station. But it grew terribly late, and I looked into the dining room at the hotel next door. Angel saw me and came to the door. She asked me to come to her table." A smile crept across her face as she remembered.

"And?"

"I don't know how she knew I was hungry, but she ordered a great amount of food. And then she said, "Oh my. I didn't mean to order so much. You'll have to help me eat it. And she even ordered coffee with real cream and sugar."

Nate eyed her, his expression gentle. "And then what, Miri?"

"And when I came back outside, we found the stage was overtaken by highwaymen and the drivers were killed. Angel talked Burton into giving me a ride here." She met his eyes, her own twinkling with amusement. "I told you it was a long story. And you, sir," she added, "are not eating."

He was halfway through his eggs now. "Go on."

"We made it almost to Pembroke when highwaymen began chasing the carriage. One of the drivers was killed; Burton was shot. I hovered down into the floorboard of the carriage until it was over because he ordered us to, and I passed out from sheer fright. But Angel... Nate, she was so brave. She shot and killed two of the men. Burton shot one, and a deputy shot and killed another." Her eyes were bright now.

"Angel did?"

"Yes. I had thought there were three, but we learned later there were four. And you won't believe this, but the fourth was the man who hired me to come to work for his mother! Of course, we didn't know that then."

Nate stopped eating and his brow rose in dismay. "You're making this up."

"I'm not," she declared firmly. "I swear."

Nate continued to stare at her. "Please tell me you didn't end up going to work for them."

She shook her head, sending her long blonde locks flying. "I didn't. The Sheriff and his posse took Angel and me to a clinic in town, but we were both kidnapped by one of the elder nurses there who supplied a local brothel—"

He choked at that, spewing his tea onto the tray, and she cupped her hand, forcefully tapping him on the back while he held a pillow to the front of his chest. Finally, he raised a hand in the air. Getting his breath, he shook his head. "I was not prepared for that one," he said, in a strangled voice. "*Dear God, child—*"

"Excuse me? I'm *not* a child," she scowled, handing him a roll and a cup of coffee. "But Lord Wellington rescued both of us; apparently just in time. She had put us behind a hidden wall where there were some extra rooms. But after we got *here—*"

"Yes." He was scowling down at her. "By all means, tell me what happened after you got *here.*"

She made a face at him. "You're goading me, Captain. Who's telling this story, anyway?"

He stared back. "Well, I swear, *miss sassylass*, there's no way under God's green earth *I* could have come up with anything like this, even if I tried—"

"Then eat and let me finish." She said with vehemence. "And then, after Angel and I recovered, I was late for my post and Lord Wellington sent them a telegram. They sent one back. They had decided against me working there, because of the stutter. He said his mother felt she couldn't bear to listen to me."

"You were so much better off. You had no business working for those people. And your mother had utterly *no* business sending you."

"Well, but at the time I had no idea what else I could do. Are you listening, Captain? Or not?"

"You have my complete and utter attention," he said, "now."

"Then be quiet and let me end my story."

"It has an ending?"

Her fist came flying toward him, and he caught her wrist deftly, as it launched toward his face.

"Whoa, little girl. That will indeed get you spanked, as surely as the sun rises in the east."

"But you're goading me."

"I admit it. I was. However, that gives you no right to propel that little fist toward me."

She stared at him. "Give me back my hand, then."

"Only if you promise to behave."

She halted, staring at him. "All right."

"Finish."

"All right. Well, there is another maid in the house that—"

"Wait—wait! What happened to Miri? We're not talking about another maid here. We're discussing *you*."

"But it's part of the story." Her expression was incredulous.

"I want to know what happened to *you*, Miri." He was becoming exasperated now. "*Is. That. Clear?*"

She sighed. "Yes. Well, we exchanged work. Angel needed a Lady's maid and I needed a simple job in the kitchen, because I had no training."

"So they gave you a job working here?"

"Yes. And Hannah, the other girl, had experience as a Lady's maid. It was actually Miss Hazel's idea that we switch." She smiled softly. "Everyone loves working here. It is a wonderful place to be. For the first time in my life, I had a nice room and plenty of food, and people who really cared about me. I'd never had that before, you see. Oh, I believe that my mother cared, but..." She shrugged. "See?"

His mouth quirked up at the corners and his eyes sparkled with mirth. "That's quite a story, Miri Clarke. And knowing you, I believe every word."

"I do not lie, Captain."

"I believe you. And if I ever should catch you attempting it, you would be quite sorry."

She sighed. "You haven't finished your food."

"I have eaten all I intend to. It was delicious."

"So," she said, her eyes sparkling, "You enjoyed inhaling the tea, as well?"

His eyes narrowed, and she couldn't help but giggle.

"You do realize, young lady, that you're asking for it. And when you get it, you'll be quite sorry."

Miri looked up at him, unsure if he was serious, or if he was jesting. Just then, however, she heard a knock at the door and went to open it. Bobby was outside with a pitcher of cool water.

"I came to pick up the tray," he said. "Please let me know if you need anything, Miss Miri."

"I shall, Bobby. Thank you. But I haven't had a chance for the sweets yet. I'll keep that one." But once he had closed the door and they were left alone, she turned to Nate. She opened her mouth to speak, but instead, tilted her head to one side and smiled.

He was asleep.

※

MIRI ADMIRED THE SCENERY AROUND HER AS NATE sat next to her in the gardens, enjoying the cool afternoon breeze. Riley, the old gardener, had brought to life a garden full of tulips in a glorious riot of color. They waved gently in the spring breeze.

Nate's arm tightened around her waist as he drew her over against his shoulder. His hands fisted in her hair as he lifted her chin upward, and his lips descended on hers.

His kiss was delectable. But her body began trembling, and she looked away.

What if Burton came around the corner?

No, Burton was resting in peace on the other side of the courtyard. Wasn't he? Something began to occur to her, and she wondered if this was real, or if it was a dream.

"Miri?" A hand descended on her hair, as a deep male voice spoke, and she jerked backward with a gasp, crying out in alarm. Her eyes were frightened; her breathing rapid and shallow.

"Miri, come here." It was Nate's voice.

Miri stared toward him for a long time before her mind registered what was happening; the gardens were gone now, and Nate was sitting before her.

She was now awake.

She shook her head, her breath still ragged, and felt her face grow hot and embarrassed as she looked up into his concerned face.

Nate moved toward the edge of the bed and pulled her over until her head rested on his shoulder. "Breathe, Miri," he said gently. "There is nothing to be afraid of. You're safe with me."

Miri turned her face downward, into his shoulder, so he couldn't see her. If her face was as red as it was hot, she knew he would demand to ask what she had dreamed.

"Oh no. You may not hide from me." But when she refused to allow him to see her face, he took hold of her hair, much as he had in her dream. "Look at me."

She shook her head, and he forced her chin upward. "Miri, I shall not allow this. Tell me what you were dreaming."

"I—I cannot—"

"Oh yes, you can." He was staring down into her eyes. "Is this the same dream that Gracie was talking about yesterday? The one that awakened the household? Have you dreamed it again?"

She shook her head as her eyes finally found his. "*No.*"

He released her hair and lowered his hand to her neck. "You may have all the time you need, Miri. But you *will* tell me."

She stared upward, defeated. Nate was not going to let this pass until she told him.

"I need to sit up." She looked away, hoping to be free of his grasp.

"As soon as you tell me."

She closed her eyes, and took a deep breath. "I dreamed," she whispered, with a gulp, "that we were in the garden, and you were—"

He waited. A moment later he murmured softly, "and I was what?"

"*Kissing* me.." It was another whisper. "A-and I kept thinking that Burton would be coming around the house and see us. And then I remembered he was," she halted, looking up into his face. "*Dead.*"

"Your eyes are mournful, sweetheart. Did you feel guilt, because we were kissing? Or sadness because you thought of Burton?"

She shook her head uncertainly. "I—I don't know."

"Would you be distressed if I kissed you?"

She felt her eyes grow wide, and blinked. "No?"

He smiled gently. "You sound quite unsure. But I won't put you in that position today." His expression was tender; his voice soothing. "Although I must admit, it's difficult for me to refrain from it." He brought her down once more to his shoulder, wrapping his arm around her. "Now, I wish to know about the nightmare that Gracie spoke of yesterday."

"No, Nate, *please*—"

"Miri, I demand to know what had you so distraught you awakened screaming. And I refuse to release you until you tell me." His voice was gentle but insistent.

She closed her eyes, immobile for a long moment.

"Take a deep breath," he whispered into her hair.

Miri fought the urge to climb into his lap, and Nate seemed to understand. He raised her higher on his shoulder; with his right arm he held her to him more closely; with his left, he guided her face into his neck until she was snuggling. She took a deep breath and relaxed.

"*I dreamt a soldier came to get me* while I was working in the hospital. He insisted I go outside. He needed my help to identify someone. He didn't say it was a body. But... I knew."

"I see."

"And when I opened the door, there was a wagon next to the walkway."

"Yes?" He was whispering into her hair, now.

"I knew what it was," she choked out. "A man's body, covered with a blanket." She let out a sob. "I knew they were bringing Burton to me to identify and I wanted to run, but I couldn't. I could only stand there and cry." She was trying to keep back the tears, but was losing her battle.

"*Miri*.." The timbre of his voice was deep and sympathetic.

"I—I cannot—"

"Yes. You can. You must. I cannot allow you to stop now. Take a deep breath."

She obeyed, breathing deeply, but when she spoke, her voice was hollow and strangled. "When they reached down to pull the blanket from his face —" She gave a wail of sorrow, and he held her very tightly to him.

"It was Burton," he said gently.

"No." Her shoulders silently shook and he tucked her further into his neck.

"*No—Nate,*" she wailed. "It was *you!*"

NATE HELD HER, SUPPORTING HER AS SHE CRIED OUT the terror and distress she felt. He whispered comforting words into her hair as he waited for her to calm. When he felt her grow limp, he leaned back onto the bed and brought her down against him once again, surprised she weighed no more than she did. He managed to lift her up onto the bed beside him, and to guide her down onto his right shoulder, still protecting his chest.

He smiled at the cascade of flaxen curls that tried to cover her face and brushed them back gently. Her delicate lashes rested against wet cheeks, and he fought against wiping them away, afraid he would awaken her. She had been through so much, this beautiful young woman.

But in his heart, he knew one thing; he wanted with all his might to take care of her; to protect her from harm, from fear, from hurt. He wanted to make her *his*. And he wanted one more thing as well.

He wanted to marry her.

They had spoken yesterday of her belonging to him. Had she truly understood that he was serious?

He would make certain she did.

꙳ 1 2 ꙳

 wakening...

A TAP ON THE DOOR CAUSED MIRI TO STIR. SHE felt hands on her face as Nate lifted it upward to meet his.

"Miri? There is someone at the door."

Her eyes fluttered open and grew wide when she realized she was lying on the bed with him. His right arm was wrapped around her as he tilted her face upward; his left was resting on her hip.

"What happened? I'm—"

"Shh, sweetheart." He patted her hip. "Go and answer it."

She pushed herself upward until she sat up on the side, and hurriedly slid down until her feet reached the floor. Looking back at him, she tried to regain her equilibrium. She took two steps toward the door before she stumbled slightly. Nate instantly reached for her.

"No—I'm all right," she whispered, embarrassed.

A moment later she opened it. Bobby was standing outside with a tray.

"I have lunches for both of you, Miss. Miri."

"Thank you, Bobby. Please come in."

By the time he got the large tray into the room over to the bed, Miri's face was an even deeper shade of scarlet. Bobby, however, set the tray down and disappeared without seeming to notice.

"Your cheeks are crimson," Nate observed, when Bobby was gone. "Is it because you fell asleep?"

She paused. "It's because I fell asleep on the bed *with you*." She retorted. "I don't even remember doing it. How did I get there?"

"I put you there."

She blinked, confused.

"You fell asleep crying against my shoulder, and I had no choice. I wasn't about to drop you on the floor, so it was necessary to bring you onto the bed with me."

She remembered, suddenly, and looked away. "I apologize."

"Don't. You don't weigh much," he teased, grinning.

"But—it's most improper to..."

"*I* won't tell anyone." His voice was deep and firm, now. "Miri, you needed me to hold you, and I was not about to let you go."

"Still—"

"*Enough,* young lady." His brows rose, and she realized he was quite serious. "Do you hear me?"

She stared. Moving back toward the tray on his lap, she began to remove the tops from the covered dishes and set them up. Nate helped, before pointing to the bed.

"Now, *sit*." He scooted over into the middle, waiting until she obeyed. "It smells wonderful. I didn't think I would be this hungry so soon after breakfast."

"Lillie is a wonderful cook," Miri acknowledged. "When I was a scullery maid, I declared I would gain weight just from working nearby and smelling it. But watching how she seasoned things helped me to know how to cook. I learned a lot from her."

The tray contained a soup, meatloaf, mashed potatoes with gravy, and green beans, and pastries on the side. "I'm surprised that we continue to have such good meals here, in spite of the war." Miri was frowning as she spoke. "Of course, much of the food comes from our garden."

She sat only long enough to pick up a few of her own dishes, and attempted to move them off to the small table.

Nate grasped her wrist with a firm hind. "Where do you think you're going?"

"I was—moving to the little table, to eat."

"No." He patted the bed next to him. "You shall eat here with me."

She eyed the bed doubtfully. "Are you sure?"

His expression turned into a scowl before her eyes. "Quite. Sit down. I must tell you, I feel stronger already. I want to take a walk this afternoon."

Miri's face filled with worry. "Nate, you're just beginning to recover."

"And I'm doing it well, thanks to your dedicated help. Don't try to keep me down, Miri. I want to fulfill the purpose I came for as soon as possible. It won't do if the Union Cavalry—*or* the Confederates —come to the door to find me propped up by a stout person on each side. They would shove me down and step over me into the house, knowing everyone here was at their mercy. Do you see?"

"I suppose, but I still worry."

"Well, stop it, sassylass."

She frowned, and her hand paused with the cover of the pastries in her hand. "Could you *possibly refrain* from calling me that?"

He eyed her as if thinking about it. "I shall consider it, but you have no idea how well it suits you."

She rolled her eyes, and he reached across and cupped her chin in his hand.

"But that expression is one you may stop. Immediately."

She opened her mouth to speak, and then bit her lip before saying, "I'll try to remember."

"It would be in your best interests." He was scowling down at her now.

Miri's gaze dropped. "You seem to enjoy threatening me," she said, frowning, as he held her chin.

"Do you think so? I assure you, little miss Miri, I do not." He sounded surprised, and after a brief glimpse up at him, she looked down once again and sighed. Nate drew a thumb across her cheek gently, before releasing her. "But I will admit something to you. I tend to forget you're not one of my men. They generally obey without question." He paused, letting his gaze roam over her face. "I'll also admit I'm quite glad you're not."

"I see."

His eyes were searching her face when she looked

up into them once again, and crinkled at the corners as he added, "And if I must explain that statement I'll be surprised at you."

Miri didn't answer; she was unable to move her gaze from his face, and he continued.

"Miri." His voice was a whisper. "I'll be honest with you, my girl. I'm enchanted with you."

She paused and blinked, still staring into his face. "I believe I'm captivated by you, too, Captain."

He leaned forward and put his hand behind her neck, drawing her to him, and brought his lips down on hers, grinning when she blinked. The tray of food between them was a barrier, keeping them from becoming too close.

His voice was extremely gentle when he spoke. "But don't forget to eat. You need some meat on your little bones. When I lifted you up onto the bed with me, I was dismayed at how light you are." When her face once again became crimson, he chuckled.

"You shouldn't have tried to lift me, sir."

His mouth quirked at the corners. "Eat," he said.

MIRI WATCHED AS HE LEANED BACK AGAINST THE headboard, after finishing his lunch. "You're exhausted," she observed.

"A bit," he said, looking down at her. "Let me rest a few moments; then I wish to get up and either sit in a chair, or go for a walk."

She nodded, and tried to take the tray from him. "Here, sir. Let me move this."

"Oh no," he said, picking it up himself and moving it to his left. Then he leaned back once again. "Sit down, Miri. We shall let Bobby have it when he comes in."

She grinned at him. "Bossy."

"Sassy," he returned. "I would order you to climb up here next to me, but it would only embarrass you further. If it bothers you to consider lying down next to me, perhaps you can rest on the chaise where I can see you."

She turned and moved toward it, sitting down and pulling up her feet.

"I could find a book to read to you in the Library," she remarked.

"And what would you choose to read?" A skeptical expression answered.

She giggled. "Well, I could borrow Merrie's copy of *Pride and Prejudice* by *Jane Austen*, and read that."

"Good Lord. Jane Austen?"

Miri ignored his statement. "But she's using it to read to the soldiers in the hall at St. Mary's, so I guess we shall have to wait on that. She says they are quite enjoying it." When he continued to stare, she hooted with laughter. "What else would you prefer? Edgar Allen Poe?" At his raised brow, she continued, "No? Hm, let us see... Perhaps Browning?"

"You may stop being facetious, Miri Clarke." He cocked his head. I'm quite sure you must have a middle name. What is it?"

She lifted her chin. "I don't think I'm inclined to tell you."

"Are you not? We shall see." Immediately, he swung his legs over the side of the bed.

Miri jumped up in alarm. "Please! You mustn't be getting up, Nate!"

"Then perhaps you'll tell me."

Her shoulders slumped. "It's Philippa," she said, her eyes downcast. "Miriam Philippa Hanner Clarke. Now, are you satisfied? And will you please lie back down?"

He continued to stare. Finally, he nodded. "I like the name Philippa. It fits you. Almost as well as *sassy-lass*." He was chuckling at her scowl. "Lie down, Miri. And so shall I." A moment later, he was flat.

Miri leaned down onto the chaise and made herself comfortable, watching him. His smile lit on her, and although his gaze rested on her, it wasn't long before his eyes drifted closed.

Miri smiled. Knowing he was asleep meant he was

comfortable; free of pain and at the moment, free of danger.

WHEN SHE OPENED HER EYES IT WAS THE FIRST thing she noticed. Nate was not in his bed, and she flew from the chaise in fright.

"Nate! Where—" But she halted as she heard the bath open and saw him coming out. "Nate! You're supposed to tell me if you need to get up!" There was anger in her voice, and he stopped, outside the door, and crooked a finger at her. Slowly she approached.

"Miri," he said quietly. "I feel very well, thank you. There are times when a man needs to relieve *by himself*. All right?"

Her face flushed and he chuckled. "Relax sweetheart. Rest assured, if I need you, I'll call. Now, if you'll accompany me to that very comfortable-looking chair over there, I'd like to sit up for a while."

Miri moved next to him, and he put an arm over her. She reached around him to steady him, and he chuckled. "Ah. I like this. I may call for your help more often."

Miri let out a giggle, and he reached down and planted a swat on her bottom.

"Teach you to laugh at me, *young lady,*" he

muttered under his breath, as another swat followed the first.

"Oh!" she cried out in surprise. "You mustn't do that. You might hurt yourself."

"Then stop laughing at me."

She helped him over to the Queen Anne chair and he lowered himself down in it carefully, patting the arm of it.

"Sit, sweetheart. This is so much better than the wooden chair at the hospital," he murmured. But when he met her eyes, she was standing back from him, and had both hands on her hips. "I'm sure you have a reason for standing there and glaring at me," he said, scowling.

"You had no right to strike me."

"Perhaps I should put you over my knee and show you the difference between striking and spanking."

She huffed out a breath and continued to stare. "I don't think there is any difference."

"Miri?" A brow rose in warning. "Would you like me to demonstrate?"

Her eyes grew wide. "*No.*"

"Then I suggest that you decide to behave properly. Or I shall give you some encouragement."

Her gaze dropped. This time, when he patted the arm of the chair, she sat.

"Much better." He said, his voice firm. "I have the distinct impression you don't believe I'll do as I say."

"It's only my worry for you. It would be so easy for you to begin bleeding inside."

He glared. "I suppose there is the possibility. Then perhaps you should work a bit harder at being obedient. And that includes refraining from sassing me."

"Perhaps. I'm sure that's true. But you can't take it personally every time I laugh, Nate."

He cocked his head. "Is that what you think? I'm taking it personally?"

She nodded.

"Hm." He studied her a moment. "Well, perhaps I am. I beg your pardon, Miri. And then again," he said, raising a brow once again, "Perhaps it's because I'd like to get my hands on your impertinent little backside for all the sass you've tossed my way since the day I met you."

"I wouldn't have been so *impertinent* if you hadn't been so difficult."

When he narrowed his eyes, she shook her head. "This is getting us nowhere, sir."

"You're quite right." He agreed, somewhat half-heartedly. "So perhaps we should back up a step, to yesterday afternoon? When we decided you would be mine?"

"Perhaps." She gave him an uncertain smile. "I would love for you to tell me more about you, and what your life was like before the war?"

"Ah. Before this dreadful war..." he rubbed his chin, feeling the stubble. "Later I'll need a mirror and a pan of soap and water in a bit. This stubble is getting to me. But for now, let me think about where I should start."

"Where did you live before the war began?"

"I grew up between the north end of Fredericksburg and Stafford. It was beautiful and unspoiled then. My parents loved each other as desperately as they loved me. My father taught me to hunt and fish, and I treasured my time with him." He paused, staring across the room.

Miri was observing him carefully as he suddenly blinked. Sensing it brought sorrow to him, she laid a hand on his arm. "You don't have to tell me if it saddens you."

Nate's gaze moved to her face. "I haven't thought of those times for a while." He smiled at her, but when it failed to reach his eyes she knew it was forced.

"When was the last time you saw your parents, sir?"

"When I left home for the war. They were killed

in 1862, during the burning. The house, I have heard still stands."

Tears were trickling slowly down Miri's face, and he smiled, reaching out to wipe them away. "You are indeed an excellent nurse, Miri. Your heart is so full of tenderness."

"I hate this war," she whispered. "*I hate it*!"

"As do I," he said softly. "You and I have both lost those dear to us. When I say I'm determined to protect you I mean every word."

But she was shaking her head vehemently. "Please, Nate, take care of yourself, too. I honestly cannot bear the thought of anything happening to you. You're not out of danger yet."

He smiled. "I know what you say is true, Miri, but I shall be very careful. You, sweetheart, are more important—"

"No, no, Nate. Can you not see? I have already lost one love. I was certain I would never have another, yet here you are." She gulped. "I cannot bear the thought of losing you, too."

He pulled her close and covered her mouth with his. "Shh, Miri. I won't have you crying. I shall be fine. And if you listen to me, so shall you."

13

T *he ground floor...*

MIRI CALLED FOR SEBASTIAN AND GLEASON LATER that afternoon at Nate's insistence. He wanted to see the ground floor of the house and stretch his legs. Miri was not at all sure about it, and she followed closely behind.

By the time he had gotten as far as the Dining room, however, he decided it was time to sit down.

"Stop hovering, Miri. I'm doing well, I think."

"If you fall on the floor from weakness, I shall leave you there, Nathan Alley." Miri was standing over him with hands on hips, glaring.

His quizzical grin incensed her even more, and she turned away in indignation just as Polly and Cissy came running into the room. The twins were followed by four older boys and two girls who looked slightly older than the twins. All of them halted abruptly in front of Nate.

Miri noticed the twins were not dressed alike today.

"You must be the soldier!" One of them said in a demanding tone.

"Yes! Miss Miri's captain!" said the other.

Grinning, Nate turned toward the first little girl. "And who might you be?"

She pirouetted before him, arms outward. "Cicely Allison Andrews."

"Ah." He turned toward the second child. "And you?"

"I," she said with a dramatic flair, "am Mary Polly Juliette Andrews."Neither of them, however, saw the boy standing behind them with curly brown hair and blue eyes, shaking his head.

"Well, it's nice to meet you, Miss Cicely," Nate said to the twin who had introduced herself as Polly, "and you too, Miss Mary Polly," he said to the other.

Both girls were indignant. Immediately they turned to look behind them.

"Abel Carter!" they both shouted at once. "Go away!"

"There you are! Cissy and Polly, back upstairs this minute!" The firm voice came from Emily, standing at the doorway. She smiled apologetically at Nate as the girls groaned and followed her orders. "I'm sorry, sir, if they bothered you."

"Oh, not at all. They were quite entertaining," he offered, "but I have yet to meet the rest of these young ladies and gentlemen."

Emily turned toward the remaining children. "You may stay long enough to introduce yourselves, but come right back up when you're finished. Geoffrey? Abel? See to it, please?" But she looked at Nate once again as she turned to go. "Please forgive my manners, sir. I'm Emily, their governess. Pleased to make your acquaintance. I must go before they get away from me again." She gave a small curtsy and disappeared.

Nate chuckled. "And who is next?"

"Lizzie?" One of the oldest boys nodded toward the girls.

"I know. There is no need for *you* to tell me what to do, Geoffrey Francis Wellington!" The taller of the girls tossed back long red curls that were tied back with ribbon, and glared at her brother indignantly. Then, putting on a sweet smile, she turned toward

Nate and gave a graceful curtsy. "I am Elizabeth Dawson Wellington, sir. But *you* may call me '*Lizzie*'. Everyone else does. My father is Lord Geoffrey Wellington, and the beautiful Lady Angel is my mother."

Nate nodded. His expression of mirth gave away the fact that he was struggling to keep from laughing. "I'm charmed, Lizzie. You look very like her. But I have only yet seen her from a distance."

The last little girl stepped forward. "I'm Katie Adams," she murmured. "Do you know my father? If so, is he all right? His name is Sir Francis Adams." She unconsciously pushed her hair back over one shoulder.

Nate's face became serious. "I must apologize, Katie, I have not met him. But I sincerely look forward to it. And you must be Merriweather's daughter? You resemble her quite strongly."

"Yes sir. Is she not very beautiful?" Katie stepped back and gave him a brief uncertain curtsey.

"Indeed, she is. And so are you, Miss Katie." He glanced over at Miri, as Katie gave him a wide smile. Miri was struggling not to laugh, as well.

"Upstairs, girls, as Miss Emily said." The tallest boy motioned toward the door. Lizzie and Katie began to move, but Lizzie stopped as she reached the doorway and turned back to Nate.

"I'm surprised Cissy and Polly didn't tell you we carry the pock here at Pembroke," she said, shaking her head. "Don't believe it, sir. They are *so dramatic*!" A toss of her curls and she was gone.

Nate looked toward the tallest boy. "The pock, hm? I shall remember that." He grinned as the boy rolled his eyes.

"I'm Geoffrey Francis Wellington, sir, as my sister said. I'm the eldest. My apologies, sir. I attempt to keep them in line, but it's very difficult. And my sister is right. We don't have 'the pock' here at Pembroke."

Geoffrey's silver eyes and dark hair were striking, Miri thought, as she watched him. So like his father.

"You appear to have your hands full," Nate said with a nod, "But thank you, Geoffrey Francis, for all you do."

The next boy who stepped forward was a younger version of his brother. "And I'm Nicholas George Wellington, sir. A pleasure to meet you. If I may help you in any way to protect the house, please tell me. I can shoot, and Papa says my aim is true."

Nate looked impressed. "Does he, Nicholas? I shall remember it, and will certainly let you know what to do." He leaned back slightly. "Do all of you know how to handle a firearm?"

"Yes, sir." All four of them nodded with pride.

"Then you shall be my back-up men," he said,

smiling. "But with your younger eyes, I may even need you to be my watchmen."

"I'm Thomas, sir." The next boy in line moved forward, seeming slightly self-conscious. "Thomas Andrews. And Cissy and Polly are my little sisters. I try to keep up with them but there are times I cannot even tell them apart. Abel is the only one who can *all* the time." He nodded toward the last boy, who was even taller than Geoffrey, and stepped back.

"They are mischievous, sir. I'm Abel Carter. And I feel sorry for Miss Emily." He was shaking his head.

Nate smiled at him. "Then I shall have to depend upon you, Abel, to help me tell them apart."

Abel nodded, smiling. "I shoot quite well, too, sir. My pa taught me."

"Very well. I should like to meet with you—all of you, and go over some safety measures starting tomorrow after school? Come down to my room when your tutoring is finished and we shall begin. Agreed?"

All four of them nodded with wide smiles across their faces, before they moved toward the doorway and made the trip back upstairs to return to class.

Miri moved to his side. "Shall I call Gleason and Sebastian to get you back to bed?"

He observed her for a moment before speaking,

and then nodded. "I think so. But I'm not exhausted, just weak. The children were delightful."

Miri only smiled as she went toward the back of the house to send for someone to escort him back to bed. Nate had been wonderful with the children, and she found herself wondering what he would be like as a father. In her mind's eye, she could almost see him, holding an infant close and smiling.

"Miri?" A voice caught her attention, and she turned, suddenly.

"Yes, Miss Hazel. The captain is ready to return to bed."

"I'll send for Gleason and Sebastian. Would you like some tea sent to the room? Lillie has made fresh scones, as well."

"That would be lovely. Thank you." Miri leaned up on tiptoe and kissed the housekeeper's cheek before leaving to go back toward the dining room. Miss Hazel stood there, watching her go with a surprised expression, and turned to go find the men.

But she was smiling.

"No telling what that child will do," she muttered under her breath.

Miri returned to the dining room, however, to find that Nate was standing up, and angrily stalked over to stand in front of him.

"Nathan Alley," she said, her voice heated, "what am I going to do with you?"

His hands descended on her shoulders. "I believe we shall talk about that very thing," he said with narrowed eyes, "later."

She was about to deliver a stinging retort when Gleason and Sebastian entered. Miri turned toward the doorway. "Thank you, sirs. Captain Alley needs to return to bed."

Both men, grinning, moved to either side of Nate, and Miri stepped away.

It would take more than a moment to calm down.

❦

When they attempted to take hold of Nate's upper arms to help him, he shook his head. "No, let me hold on to you," he said firmly. "Tell me. Has little miss Miri always been this sassy?"

Gleason just chuckled. Sebastian, however, laughed openly. "You should have seen her when she came here. Meek as a mouse. Took Burton a long time to release her from her shell."

"Hm." They had reached the green room, and Nate's voice was more of a grumble as he sat down on the edge of the bed and pushed himself backward.

"Thank you, gentlemen, for your help. I don't think I could have made it back alone."

But as they disappeared, he leaned back against the headboard, scowling.

A moment later, Miri stood inside the door. She was scowling, too.

He watched her for a minute, and then turned to her and motioned, patting the side of the bed. "Come here." He said, his tone fierce.

She did not move.

"Miri? Must I come and get you?"

"No."

"Obey me, then."

She stared at him a moment longer, and then sighed, and moved closer. But she stopped before she got there, just out of his reach.

"Sit."

Still, she stayed where she was.

"Miriam Philippa Clarke. Is it your desire to try my patience?"

"No."

"Then what is it you're attempting to do?"

"I'm trying," she said, glowering, "to take care of you and nurse you back to health. But you're fighting me, sir, at every turn."

He held out his hand toward her, and she stared at it.

"Young lady, if I have to come and get you, I shall."

Miri blinked and raised her eyes to his. He was utterly serious. When she finally rested her hand in his, Nate closed his fingers around her wrist and tugged her toward him. His right hand curled into her hair, bringing her to his shoulder.

"Can you not let me heal on my own terms, child?"

"I'm not a child."

"Then you may stop behaving like one. I feel very good. Endurance is my only challenge now. And you must stop scowling at me every time I try to increase it. By doing so, you challenge me further."

She raised her head, looking into his face. "Do you truly think so?"

He nodded. "I do. And you haven't answered my question."

Her face was so close to his, yet he didn't release her hair, and brought her even closer.

"I... don't remember what it was." She whispered.

"I asked if you can let me heal on my own terms." His lips touched hers, and his tongue invaded her mouth, dancing with hers. Miri's eyes were wide now, and he smiled. Reaching around her with his left arm, he crushed her against him.

Miri began to feel weak; by the time he let her go,

she was trying to hold herself up on the side of the bed and fearing her legs would not support her.

A hand reached down and swatted her bottom lightly, and she gasped.

"Answer me, Miri."

Her eyes met his, clearly confused, and he chuckled. "You forgot it again when I kissed you."

She gave a slight nod.

"Never mind, sassylass. Now I know just how to silence you when you get out of hand."

A knock sounded at the door. Still, Miri didn't move for a moment. When it sounded again, her eyes flew open wide. Nate let her go.

"Perhaps you'd better answer that."

She nodded and hurried toward the door. Gracie stood in the hall, dancing with excitement. "General Sheridan is marching his troops through town toward Woodstock," she said, flying into the room. "I knew you would wish to know that, Captain!"

Nate's scowl answered. "Through town?"

"Yes. I heard some of the soldiers saying that Early's army couldn't withstand another siege and they thought the war was soon to end. But we saw them on the way home, too. A lot of them."

Nate frowned, blinking. "Thank you, Gracie. Do you mind bringing in all the ladies? Now?"

"Yes, sir. I'll be right back. I believe Miss Hazel is preparing tea. Shall I have her just bring it in here?"

But Miri had already run out into the hallway and began urging all the others into the room. She saw Bobby coming with a large tray and ran ahead of him, pulling one of the little tables into the center of the room.

"I shall pour, Bobby. Thank you." Miri smiled, realizing there were enough cups and saucers and scones for everyone. She began handing out cups and saucers and filling them with the hot, steamy, pungent liquid. She took the captain his cup, and offered him one of the tarts from the tray.

As he took it, his fingers brushed hers; Miri gave a small gasp as she felt the tingling sensation that crept up her hands. Their eyes met, and he winked at her.

A tiny smile escaped her lips, and she turned away, embarrassed. Gracie had finished pouring and all of them were settled.

"So, ladies," Nate's quiet, rich voice said as he looked from one to the other of them. "Please share with me what you saw today?"

One at a time, they told him, from their own points of view. Angel had overheard some of the conversation among some of the men as she went outside to see what was going on. They had discussed going after Early's army, and said Sheridan was sure to win.

Merrie had stopped her reading to run upstairs to the upper floor of the church. She had listened to a Commanding Officer as he spoke with another, and had gone back to relay what she'd seen to the injured soldiers in the hall who were unable to see what was happening. The army was on their way to Woodstock.

Nate listened, glancing down at Miri, as they spoke about their day. They had actually left the hospitals early to make it home. Only Mollie had stayed.

"We wanted to make sure everything was safe here." Gracie added.

Nate leaned his head back and relaxed, closing his eyes, as the ladies of the house left the room. Miri brought out the tray and set it outside the door, and went back in to observe him. His breathing was deep now; his brow relaxed. He had not asked for anything for pain all day long. Miri had offered it once and he had declined, scowling at her. She hoped he would ask if he needed it.

Hoping he would sleep for a bit, she sneaked out of the room and found the others.

Angel spoke first. "Miri, we need a plan, in case some of the soldiers show up at the house tonight."

Miri frowned. "I'm sure the captain is considering what to do," she said thoughtfully. "Do we have our weapons and our ammunition ready?"

When Ellie shook her head, followed by Merrie, Gracie spoke up. "Mine is. Shall we all go upstairs to ready them? I can help." She turned to look toward Miri, who nodded.

"I think so. And bring mine down, please, Gracie? I think perhaps we should all sleep down here tonight after the children go to bed. I have a feeling Nate is going to order me to sleep upstairs tonight. But I have an idea. This is what I think we should do…"

14

t the ready...

NATE SLEPT ONLY FOR AN HOUR. WHEN HE awakened, he immediately looked around for Miri, to find her sitting in the shadows, peeking through the curtains.

"What do you see?" He was watching her profile, silhouetted against what light was still outside the window. "Be careful, Miri. If there are troops outside, they mustn't see you watching them."

"Yes, sir, I know, but I'm trying to be careful. There are some shadows, Nate. I cannot tell if they are cast by soldiers; only figures; they're not far from the house."

"Is that a rifle, I see?"

She turned to him. "Yes. But Nate," she paused. "There is no way you can fire a rifle right now—the kick would probably rip something loose and you could begin to bleed."

Nate was watching her face. She was terribly worried; unfortunately, he also knew she was right. If he were to bleed to death, his job as protector of the household would be over; so would the safety of Pembroke.

"Then let us pray I don't need to use it." He said.

Tears began to trickle down Miri's cheeks, and he rose, holding on to the bedpost. His legs felt strong. His chest didn't.

Miri immediately flew to meet him, and he said softly, "Walk with me to the window, sassy."

She wrapped her arms around his waist, and he rested his arm on her shoulders, sitting back down on the chaise that sat in front of the window.

"Where did you see them?"

"On the other side of the brook, where the curved bridge crosses it. Can you see?"

He watched for a moment. "I see. You're right; there are many out there, but they don't look as if they're watching the house. They seem to be busy going about their own business. It could be that they are just waiting until darkness falls to approach."

"I've asked the girls to ready their weapons—and the ladies in the staff wing are doing it as well. All of us can shoot, Nate. Even the young boys. Very well."

Nate traced a finger down the descending tear on her face. "As much as I would prefer that you be upstairs and away from this, I see little choice for tonight. I want to know what others are seeing from the higher windows. The boys might be in a suitable position to watch from the third floor. Possibly even Lizzie and Katie could help from up there."

"Yes. Shall I arrange it?"

He studied her small face. "Yes. I'll watch from here until you return."

Miri attempted to rise, but he caught her braid in his hand, pulling her face to his. The kiss he planted on her lips was deep and powerful. Her heart was pounding and her breath was shallow when he finished and let her up.

"Go," he said softly.

❧

THE FIRST THING MIRI NOTICED THAT EVENING when she walked into the dining room was the buffet.

"Where is the blue lamp?" She asked, her gaze immediately moving to Angel.

Angel smiled. "I decided to put it away until peace time. It's too valuable for me to risk leaving it out in the present situation. I'll put it back when a treaty is signed, in its original spot next to the piano."

Miri only nodded. "I understand. Perhaps it's best." She took her seat next to Nate, who was already at the end.

Supper was quiet; they all looked from one to the other. The children had eaten, and were getting ready for bed by eight, but only Cissy and Polly fell asleep, apparently unaware that anything was going on. As soon as they were asleep, Katie and Lizzy nodded toward each other and went to their places to watch.

The upper windows were manned by the younger children; Katie and Lizzie went into Angel's room to watch toward the brook, while Thomas kept an eye on the graveyard on the other side. The moon was up now, and it was easier for him to spot shadows against the snow.

Nicholas, keeping his pistol by his side went toward the back of the house to watch toward the woods and the yews near the pond, and Geoffrey Francis and Abel descended the staff stairway and went through the hallway to the second-floor rooms. Geoffrey Francis observed from the front of the house, while Abel perched at the top of the stairway, his pistol handy. The staff wing was equally prepared.

Nate had called them all to him, explaining the dangers present and the precautions needed, until he was satisfied everyone knew exactly what to do. Miri, he had tugged down next to him, holding onto her hand as he searched her face.

He lifted her chin so bring her face up to his. "Is there any possible way I can get you to go upstairs, out of danger?"

Miri was cautious with her answer. "Nate, I'm strong and healthy and a good shot. You just had surgery. There is no way I could make myself leave you or the others down here alone. If you were better, and stronger—"

"If I were, I would not allow you to disobey my orders. But I do understand. *This time*."

She smiled up into his eyes. "Could you close your eyes and rest for a while? I shall wake you if anything happens." But she lowered her gaze and bit her lip as she saw the expression on his face. "The truth is this, Captain Nathan Alley," she said, leaning forward and kissing him softly

"Right now, you need me."

IT WAS 2:00 A.M. WHEN ABEL, FROM THE TOP OF the steps, said in a voice, just loud enough for them to be able to hear on the ground floor.

"Geoffrey thinks they are coming toward the front porch!"

They waited.

"Everyone ready?" Nate's deep male voice asked quietly.

"Ready," they answered, all at the same time.

A vicious pounding on the front door caused Miss Hazel to turn toward Nate.

"*Now?*"

"Now."

She moved toward the door, tapping her cane on the hardwood with her left hand, her right hand in her pocket, ready. Miri and Nate could see her as she took a deep breath and opened the door.

"Sergeant Friberg, Union Cavalry, ma'am. The Army hereby commandeers this property for its use." He made a move as if to shove her backward, but Miss Hazel stepped away, moving back into the hallway of the left wing. The Sergeant moved forward with his men, creating a line inward. He stopped before it branched off to each of the wings. Nate was perched on the back of a chair by now, directly in front of him, rifle in hand.

"I don't think so, Sergeant." Nate's answer was

firm and strong. "You may turn around and leave the way you came in."

The Officer halted, along with his men.

"Who says?" he said, obviously surprised.

Nate's large frame looked down on him from fifteen feet away. This time, his voice was dictatorial. "*We* do."

The long pause caused the silence to sound utterly deafening.

"And…" There was another pause before Friberg spoke, "Who are you? And who is 'we?'"

"Captain Nathan Alley. And perhaps you should light a lantern, Sergeant, so that you may see *my* army."

Friberg huffed out a laugh of disbelief. Then he turned toward the door. "Bring a lantern!" he shouted.

From outside, a soldier carried in a lantern. He stopped as he neared them. The Sergeant nodded toward him. "Move forward, Private."

"No, Private," Nate barked. "Stand back. A leader worth his salt does not ask another to stand between him and danger. He takes the responsibility of doing it himself."

The Sergeant's anger was palpable as he moved over and took the lantern from the Private.

But he had taken only five or six steps into the

room, approaching Nate, when he began to see them. Every two feet stood a woman, dressed in her night-gown and holding a weapon aimed directly at them. Each of Friberg's soldiers had at least six weapons trained on him. Miss Hazel, when he spotted her, was standing in perfect form, with her weapon aimed right at his heart.

Even in the dim lantern light, the Sergeant's eyes were enormous.

"You see, Sergeant," Nate's voice echoed in the large room, "This house is full of people who have had their homes confiscated by one army or the other. They would not hesitate to dispose of you and every single one of your men before letting it happen again."

The silence that followed seemed to last an eternity.

Finally, the Sergeant cleared his throat. "I... had no idea you were here, Captain. Or we would not have disturbed you." He nodded toward his men with an order to retreat, and they began to file slowly back out. Miss Hazel followed him to the front door, counting the soldiers who had departed, so she knew each of those that had entered had also gone. She closed the door and bolted it behind them.

A collective sigh of relief was heard over the entire room.

"Well done, ladies," Nate said, nodding toward them, and then glanced up at Abel, still perched on the top step. "And gentlemen. I'm extremely proud of you. But don't leave yet. I know of Sergeant Friberg. We have embarrassed him, and it would not surprise me if he returned. Perhaps not tonight, but don't let down your guard. I realize it's late. If you're exhausted, you may leave and get some sleep. If not, find a spot and make yourself comfortable, but keep your weapon nearby and ready."

Geoffrey Francis came to rest on the top step next to Abel.

"Captain Alley, they are leaving, sir. They seem to be departing toward the road. And Katie and Lizzie say that the ones near the bridge are following."

"It is the same here, from the other side of the house." Hannah added from the staff wing.

"Good. If they're leaving by the road, we may be all right for tonight. Still, remain vigilant. It could very well be a trick." He lowered himself down onto the long sofa and sat down, motioning Miri to come and sit beside him.

"Bring Abel and Geoffrey Francis to me, Miri. Please?"

She nodded with a big smile and went to find them. They were both still at the top of the steps, and followed her down the stairs, quietly.

Nate, when he saw them, reached out a hand and rested it on each boy's shoulder. "I wanted to thank you, gentlemen. Because of you, we were all ready, and everything went off perfectly as planned. We thank you for being so diligent, and for letting us know they were here. Everyone did their part. Thank you, and please tell the others I would like to see them, too."

Both boys were beaming when they went back upstairs to fetch the others. Nicholas and Thomas, and then Katie and Lizzie, and the children from the staff wing who had been watching, tiptoed down so Nate could speak to them. Miss Hazel too, he praised her for her role in answering the door.

It was nearly four when the household calmed down. Miri fell asleep against Nate's shoulder, and he moved her so her head was in his lap while he remained on alert. He reached down to touch her soft hair and gently pulled it away from her face, watching as the firelight played across her profile. She would be terribly embarrassed when she awakened and realized she was resting in his lap.

MIRI STIRRED IN HER SLEEP. HER DREAMS WERE vivid but not unsettling, and when she finally opened her eyes it was daylight. She looked down to see Nate's left arm resting protectively around her; his right rested gently on her hair. She tried to turn onto her back unsuccessfully; then she tried to sit up; that didn't work either; Nate's hands only tightened around her. His right hand fisted tightly in her hair when she attempted to move.

"Nate?"

A grumble escaped. He was obviously asleep. She grinned, repeating, "Nate!"

When his eyes finally opened, he stared down at her.

"I need to get up," she said softly.

He blinked, looking around the room before moving his hand from her waist and smoothing her hair gently.

"Thank you," she whispered. "May I help you back to bed?"

"Do you mind checking out the front window in the great room first? Carefully, Miri. Don't let anyone see you."

She rose, and he caught her wrist. "Good girl. Thank you."

She ran to the great room window. From the corner where the piano sat, she could see out both windows. There were no signs of any soldiers present.

"The west and the north are clear as best I can tell."

"Good." He leaned forward, pushing himself up to a standing position, and groaned.

"Oh! You're hurting," she said, her voice full of sympathy.

"No. I'm stiff, that's all." He pulled her to him and wrapped an arm about her shoulders to steady himself.

When he got back into bed, however, he leaned backward onto the headboard and closed his eyes.

"Sleep, Nate," she said, softly. "I'm awake now."

"For just a bit. But promise me to wake me if anything occurs."

"Yes, sir. I shall."

"Sit here, next to me for a moment." He reached for her hand. But this time, instead of grasping her wrist as if not to allow her to get away, he took her hand in his and held it.

She watched his face as he relaxed and looked down at his hands. Such big, strong hands. She thought of the voice he had used the night before when the Sergeant had entered the house. That authoritative voice would have scared her away too. Now, however, he looked like a little boy, with his curly hair tousled around his face.

She tiptoed quietly into the hallway, and then

from room to room to check on the rest of the household. Angel and Merrie were up, and had sent the others to get some sleep. The children were resting now, except for Abel. He was roaming from room to room on the third floor, watching down on the different areas around the grounds.

Then Miri moved over to the staff wing. Things were much the same. Hannah Kimbrow claimed not to be sleepy in the slightest, and Sheila Carter, along with Bobby, were prowling the house and keeping an eye outward on the property.

Realizing how exhausted she was, Miri tiptoed back into the bedroom, putting her hand back into Nate's. He opened his eyes briefly, and then pulled her closer to him, clasping her hands in his once again.

Slowly, a wave of sleepiness overtook her, and she fought it, not wanting to remove her hand from his. But eventually, she found she could sit up no longer. She moved over to the window. The sun was up, now, and she looked out toward the east. All was clear as far as she could see.

Miri stretched out on the chaise and pulled the throw over her, before lying back and allowing her eyes to drift closed.

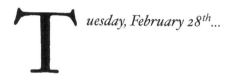

15

T uesday, February 28th...

IT WAS SEVEN A.M. WHEN BOBBY KNOCKED ON THE door. But instead of bringing breakfast, he said only, "Miss Hazel said breakfast will be served in the dining room in a half-hour, Miss Miri. She said if the captain was unable to come, she would have his sent here."

"Thank you, Bobby. Did you get some sleep?"

"Yes, ma'am. After we got back to bed, I slept quite soundly."

"Good. I shall be in the dining room. I'm not sure about the captain."

"Yes, ma'am," he said, once again.

Miri turned back to look at Nate, surprised to find his eyes on her, and a brow raised.

"You're awake," she said, "I'm surprised. I didn't expect it."

"I'll eat in the dining room with the rest of you. It's important." He looked toward the door to the bath. "I believe I need to wash up."

"Do you need someone to help?" she asked, then let out a giggle at his returned expression.

"You may walk with me to the door. I believe this is a chore I must take care of by myself." He stopped and gave her a wink outside the door. "This is as far as you go, sassylass. Upstairs with you. I shall be ready when you get back."

"And I shall wait right here until you're finished."

He frowned. "Miri." His voice was full of warning. "Go."

"After you're out," she repeated.

He stared down at her, his scowl deepening. "Miriam Philippa, I'd rather not have to spank you this morning. Go upstairs and get ready. Now."

She looked up. At the tone of his voice, she realized just how serious he was. She could feel her eyes widen, and she turned on her heel and walked toward the bedroom door without looking back.

When she realized how forcefully she had

slammed it behind her, she stopped and closed her eyes. Then she shook her head and rushed for the stairs.

It took her only a few moments to change. Gracie had washed up and was about to go downstairs.

"How is our captain?" she said, curiously.

"In the bath. And he demanded that I leave the room. If he passes out, it's his own fault."

Gracie grinned. "You two are indeed a pair, do you realize that? Here. I shall fix your hair after you freshen up. But hurry."

Miri grumbled constantly as she visited the wash basin, and was still muttering under her breath when Gracie helped her with the corset and fastening of her gown.

"For pity's sake, Miri, *be still*. I shall never be able to get your hair done if you keep moving about."

But even after uttering thanks to Gracie for her help, Miri was still disgruntled. She descended the staff stairway and entered the dining room through the kitchen, waving at Lillie and Miss Hazel as she passed.

Miss Hazel eyed her curiously. "Breakfast will be served in three minutes, my girl," was all she said.

"Yes, ma'am." Miri stopped abruptly as she saw Nate seated at the end of the table, dressed in his fresh uniform.

She let out a long breath as he rose to seat her next to him. "Good morning again," he said.

"Good morning, Captain," she tossed back , more than a little coldly. "I didn't expect to find you in here already." She was not smiling when she spoke, and when she glanced up at him neither was he. His brow was raised in warning.

Miri looked away quickly.

The exchange was not lost on Angel, who sat on Miri's other side. She looked around the table and asked brightly, "Who is going to the hospital today? I am."

"I am," Ellie spoke up. "I'm taking some paper to write letters for the soldiers—as many as possible."

"There is extra paper in Geoffrey's study," Angel offered. "I'll get it for you before we leave."

"I'm going to immerse them further in Jane Austen." Merrie was grinning now."

"You two are getting all the fun tasks," Angel said as she rolled her eyes. "But someone has to do what Gracie and I do."

Gracie was grinning. "But Miri does it better than anyone. I think Dr. Foster regrets firing her. And I feel bad because it was partly due to me. Anyway, I shall go today, too."

One by one they left the table, stopping to give Miri a hug and to say goodbye to the captain. Miri watched them go. For the first time, she had the courage to bring her eyes up to meet his.

Nate was staring down at her, his brow knit into a frown, when he rose from the table. He held out his hand. "Come with me, young lady."

There was a long hesitation before Miri let her hand rest in his. With one hand holding hers and the other at the small of her back, Nate led her back to the room.

A moment later he sat down on the edge of the chaise and took her by the waist, drawing her to stand between his thighs. He studied her for a few moments before he spoke.

Miri remained silent as she waited. His gaze wasn't angry; she was glad of that. But it was determined.

"Look at me, Miri." he said, lifting her chin with one hand. "What did you think you were doing, storming out of the room and slamming the door in a fit of temper?"

She blinked rapidly. "I... didn't really mean to slam it," she said, with a gulp. "I was upset and worried."

"That was more than just being upset. That was a show of temper, if ever I saw one." He turned her face upward. "Who has temper tantrums, Miri? Tell me."

She lowered her gaze. "Children," she whispered.

"That's right," he said, staring down at her. "I know I've referred to you as a child in the past, but you've always been quick to inform me you're not."

She shook her head silently.

"And I've I also explained," he added, "when you behave this way, you're in danger of discipline. Didn't I?"

Her eyes flew to meet his. "Oh, Nate. I'm so afraid you'll hurt your chest if you try."

"I'm capable of being careful not to do that," he said gently. "There is a wooden measuring rod in the umbrella stand by the door in the bath. Bring it to me."

She gasped, but did not move. She could feel her eyes widen as she stood there, shaking her head. "Please... Nate. *No..*"

"Either you can bring it, or I'll get it myself, young lady. You'd be wise to obey me."

Miri wasn't sure she could get her feet to move. What if he pulled something loose? What if he began to bleed? Pembroke was so far away from the hospital. What if...

"Miri Philippa." His voice was calm as he turned her and sent her forward. "Now, please."

A tear escaped and made its way down her cheek as she moved slowly toward the bath. Once inside the door, she looked around. Nate was right; in the corner was an umbrella stand, and inside it stood two umbrellas, a cane and the measuring rod. Miri reached for it with shaking hands and pulled it from the stand.

Her eyes closed for a moment in dread, and she leaned against the wall. Tears began falling more rapidly.

She had no idea how long she had rested there, but suddenly, the door to the bath opened and closed again. Nate was standing over her, and her chest began to heave more rapidly.

"Miri, you need not fear me, but it's necessary to show you that you're held accountable for your actions when you show temper, as you did this morning." He held out his hand for the ruler, and she surrendered it.

"But I fear you will further damage your injury, sir..." she whispered.

"I'll use my wrist." He leaned forward and kissed her forehead before taking her arm and leading her over to the table beside the sink. "Bend over the table and rest your arms on it. Clasp your hands together."

A small sob choked from her as she made herself obey. Her hands finally rested on top, near the sink, and he gently put a large hand on her back and encouraged her to bend forward a little more. She clasped her hands together, fighting to still her trembling.

But when he began to raise her skirts she gasped, and tensed. Her eyes grew immensely wide as she met his eyes in the mirror.

"Tell me, sweetheart," he said. "Why is this happening to you?"

"Because.." she whispered, "I-I acted out in temper..."

"And?"

"I-I s-slammed the door."

"Are you allowed to slam doors in a fit of temper, Miri?"

She shook her head. "No."

"And is this the first time you have acted out and shown your temper?"

She swallowed, hard. "No, sir."

"No. Nor is it the first time I have discussed with you the fact that when I became stronger, you would be taken across my knee for a spanking. I wish you to count with each swat. Do you understand?"

Miri closed her eyes. "Yes, sir." She took a sharp breath as the rest of her skirts and petticoats were brought up over her back.

When the first blow landed she was stunned. She shrieked in surprise and began to breathe sharply, rapidly. Her head came up, and she blinked, looking into the mirror and meeting his eyes. His were determined; her own were showing frightened betrayal.

"Count, Miri."

"O—*one*.." It was barely audible, but it was there.

She saw his hand raise slightly in the mirror, and closed her eyes, waiting. When it fell, it brought forth another cry.

"*Two*.."

He began lecturing, quietly, firmly, as she cried out the number following each one.

"Tell me, Miri," he said, after the sixth one, "is this what you need to help you remember to behave and mind your manners?"

"Six, sir," she was weeping softly now.

Another fell, and she cried out again.

"Answer me. Is this what it will take?"

"I—I don't—know!" Her voice broke with a sob.

"What number was that, Miri?"

She tried to remember. "S—seven—*sir*?" She answered, unsure she was right.

He leaned forward and kissed the back of her neck softly. "Three more to go, sweetheart."

A wail escaped, and she rested her head on her hands.

The next two fell in rapid succession. Miri whispered the numbers, and Nate leaned toward her once again, and spoke into her ear in a deep voice.

"Only one more, Miri. Do you think you can remember, from now on, not to slam doors and flounce away?"

"Yes, sir," she cried out in a sob.

"All right. This is the last. Brace yourself."

When it landed, she let out a wail, and collapsed onto her arms on the table, weeping. Her "Ten" took multiple tries before she was successful.

She knew she'd been temperamental this morning; she had also been cross with him on several other occasions, even at the hospital. And she thought of the time that he had caught her wrist as she sent her fist toward his face. She vowed never to do it again.

Nate reached under her and lifted her as he smoothed her skirts downward again. She found herself pulled into his embrace, sobbing into his chest with her head tucked under his chin. One of his hands held her to him; the other was wrapped into her hair.

"I'm sorry, sir," she whispered. "*I'm so sorry.*"

"Shh," his voice said into her ear. "You're forgiven, and I'm hoping we can have a quiet and pleasant day today. But I want you to remember this, my darling girl." His voice was soft, but there was a slight hint of warning there, too. "Because the next time you act out in temper, it'll be worse for you."

She nodded under his chin.

He dropped the wooden measuring rod into the stand, and then led her back out into the room and over to the Queen Anne chair, and guided her into his lap. Leaning her back against his shoulder, he cradled her, letting her continue to cry.

"Cry, sweetheart. Cry it out."

Miri wrapped her arms around his chest as the dam seemed to burst. Cries turned back into sobs as she let go of the pent-up sorrows over the years; the nightmares, the long days of seeing the death and destruction of the never-ending war; the loss of her dearest Burton. She'd never allowed her grief to show, for so many others had the same heartaches. Years of sorrow escaped in great wailing sobs, until it seemed there was nothing more to release.

Her cries became softer as Nate held her to him. Miri wearily let her arms rest around his neck until sleep eventually overtook her.

THE GONG OF THE GRANDFATHER CLOCK IN THE great room pierced her consciousness, and she opened her eyes. What had it said? Was that two chimes? One? She glanced up, realizing she was in Nate's lap.

He was grinning down at her, and she sat up in his

lap, suddenly, with a sharp breath. "How long have I been here?"

He took hold of her arm. "Watch those little elbows," he said, brows raised.

"I'm sorry. What time is it?"

"It's two o'clock. Bobby brought lunch at noon."

Her expression showed distress. "I've been sleeping all this time?"

"Yes, and you cried your heart out. I think you must have needed it. And later, I'd like to hear about it. Those sobs were about more than just the fact that I spanked you."

She looked away, and a moment later, nodded.

"Here. Let's see what the tray contains."

"You should have awakened me."

"I think not. You needed sleep more than I needed food." He helped her to stand.

When Miri lifted the covers from the tray, the contents were still warm; crisp beef and Swiss sandwiches, with tomato bisque soup and some cherry scones served with tea. Lillie's chunky apple sauce was in a little bowl on the side. She edged the tray over so they could both eat.

"I'd like to try a stroll once more around the ground floor, Miri. It ended sooner yesterday than I intended."

She swallowed a bite of sandwich, and then said, thoughtfully. "Are you rested enough, sir?b"

"Well rested. I slept while you did. And if I give out on strength, I know now where the chairs are. I can always sit down." He reached out and tugged on a lock of her hair. "Tell me. Did your sleep help you?"

She nodded. "It did. I feel much better."

"Good, then." He reached out and tucked a stray strand of hair behind her ear. "Eat, so we may go for a walk."

She paused abruptly, staring at him.

"Miri? What is it?"

She swallowed. "Did—did Bobby bring the tray in while I was asleep? In—in your lap?"

Nate grinned. "You prefer I put you down on the floor at my feet and leave you while he came in? I was not about to do that. Bobby is discreet; he didn't seem at all surprised. The only thing we discussed was the intrusion last night. He watched from the window in the left wing. He's getting some sleep today, so he may watch again tonight if needed."

She looked up at him. "You think they might come back tonight?"

He heaved a sigh. "There's no way to know. I wish I could ride, so I could make a trip to town and see what's truly going on. The Cavalry may have moved southward to be with the rest of the army. The Confederates at Merriweather's house may be prisoners of war now and may also be gone. It's a pain being unable to get about."

"Perhaps tomorrow, if you're up to it, we could have Benjamin take us both into town in the carriage? It would give you a chance to get out." She paused. "And you know better questions to ask than I."

"Perhaps. I like that idea."

It was an hour later when Abel came flying down the steps from the east wing.

"A soldier's coming toward the house," he said, breathlessly, "on a horse!"

"Only one, Abel?"

"Yes, sir. Alone."

Miri rose to answer it, and Nate put a restraining hand on her shoulder.

"No. I shall answer it. But bring my rifle, please."

Miri hurried in with it, along with the pistol Burton had left her. Miss Hazel came forward with her weapon in her pocket.

"Shall I answer it for you, Captain?"

Nate spoke thoughtfully. "I believe I shall do it this time, Miss Hazel. However, if you want to stand with Miri and back me up, I shall be grateful. Let's see what he wants." He went to the door and opened it.

A young Union soldier was standing alone outside

the door. He looked barely sixteen. There was a sling on his right arm, and a cast could be seen protruding from it. In his left, he carried a bag. "Hello, sir. Private Killian. I carry mail with me. Is this Pembroke?"

"It is, Private."

"Good, then. I have posts for the residents from my unit east of Harper's Ferry."

Miri stepped to the side, peeking around Nate.

"Do you serve with Geoffrey Wellington or Francis Adams, sir?"

"I did, ma'am," he was nodding. "You know them?"

"Yes!"

Nate frowned down at Miri and finally spoke above her head. "Come in, Private Killian. I have a feeling this young lady won't allow to leave until you've answered her questions. Do you carry a weapon?"

A remorseful expression crossed the young man's face. "I do, sir, but it's the devil to get to, and my left-handed aim is poor. My home is Winchester, but many of the soldiers in my unit were from the Shenandoah Valley. They sent mail to be delivered, and I wished to get it to you as soon as possible." He followed Nate inside, with a limp.

"You're hurt, sir," Miri observed.

"No ma'am. I *was* hurt. I'm nearly well, but they tell me I cannot continue to serve with this leg and arm."

"Sit down, sir," Miss Hazel said softly. "Would you take tea with us?"

"Oh, yes ma'am. I'd be delighted."

Nate led them into the great room and motioned for the soldier to sit. "You said you bear posts."

Killian smiled. "Quite a few. May I?" He looked toward Nate, who nodded.

A moment later, the bag he carried was turned upside down, flooding the table with envelopes that spilled over onto the floor. Miri gave a delightful giggle as she retrieved them. She put them into stacks divided only by the family wing and the staff wing, and began moving toward the latter.

Hannah Kimbrow met her on the stairs. She broke into a run as she spotted the posts in Miri's hands. "Miri!" She cried out in delight. "Did you happen to see any of them from Adam?"

"Oh, Hannah, there are so many. But I believe I did. These are for your wing. Can you help me go through them and pass them out? The rest are for the other wing. I believe I saw—" Miri stopped. Hannah was no longer hearing a word she said; she was digging through them excitedly, looking for ones from her husband.

"Three!" A huge smile broke out on Hannah's face, and she leaned forward, kissing Miri on the cheek. "Thank you, Miri! I'll pass the rest of these out before I read mine. Oh—wait! " She turned to Miri, excited. "Lady Angel and Lady Angel will be so thrilled! It's been so long..."

And she was gone.

Miri laughed and turned to go back down the stairs. When she next saw Miss Hazel come into the great room with the tea tray, Miri handed her the posts for her friends. "There are four each, from Geoffrey and Francis for Angel and Merrie," she said, grinning. "Do you wish to do the honors when they get home?"

Miss Hazel smiled at her. "I shall put them next to their dinner plates." She was chuckling now. "They should be home soon."

Miri again reached Nate's side, and he took hold of her arm and pulled her down next to him.

"Sit, Miri. Private Killian is telling me what's happening in town."

The young soldier turned to Miri. "I came from the north, ma'am, but this is what I understand from other troops. Sheridan is moving the troops on down today to New Market. There weren't as many troops in town today as I came through. Some of the houses occupied by Union forces now sit empty. The hospitals are still full, of course. Captain Alley told me about the troops that paid you a visit during the night. They may no longer be here. But as I passed —" he paused, as excited female voices filled the room, and looked behind him.

Angel, Merrie, and Gracie entered the great room as Nate spoke. "Come in, ladies, and meet Private Killian. I believe this young man served with your husbands. I thought you might have some questions for him."

They all began speaking at once.

"Is Francis eating enough?"

"Is he well?"

"Are they anywhere near here?"

"Is Geoffrey terribly homesick?"

"Did they send a post?"

"Have you seen William?"

Their voices fell over each other in their quest for information, and finally, Nate put up a hand.

"One at a time, please?"

Killian answered their questions as best he could. But he had yet more news. He had passed the Adams house on the way and had seen a few Union Cavalry there. When Merrie asked about the condition of the house, he was vague.

Miri met Nate's eyes while everyone else spoke. She was so delighted that her friends had received letters; more delighted still, that they were able to get first-hand information from someone who had served with their husbands. This meant all of them had gotten a post within the past few weeks.

Finally, the young soldier rose to leave, politely declining an invitation to stay for supper. "Thank you, but I must go."

Miri approached him as he moved toward the door. "Thank you, sir. You have made our ladies indeed very happy today."

"It put a smile on my face too, ma'am," he said.

❧ 16 ❧

T *he posts...*

SQUEALS AND LAUGHTER FILLED THE DINING ROOM when the ladies approached the dinner table and sat down to see their letters waiting for them. Miri's eyes were sparkling, when she looked up to see Nate. He was grinning down at her, the corners of his mouth upturned as well.

Angel pulled hers out and opened the top one on the stack, her worried eyes peering down at it. She looked around at the others, seated at the table.

"Please, everyone, go ahead and eat. I shall take these to the Ladies' Parlor to read them."

Merrie did the same, going instead, to the great room.

She pulled out Francis' letter, doing as Gracie had done and reading the last one first. She smiled, when she read his greeting.

"*Dearest Merriweather,*

My darling little miscreant, how I miss you! I know it's been two months since you and Angel heard from Geoffrey and I, yet I promise you there is a reason. We're on special duty at present; this is the first time either of us has dared to write, due to the extreme secrecy required for this mission. If they had gotten into the wrong hands previously, it might have endangered and changed the outcome of the entire war.

Yet, now there is slightly less danger, and we both feel that it's safe to get in touch with you. Our mission is soon to be over; there is indeed hope that the war may soon be over, as well.

How is little Katie? I thank you so much for the likeness that Gracie drew of the two of you. Our darling daughter is so like you, I see your face and mannerisms in her with each glance. How a man can say he only wants sons is beyond me; Katie is so precious. I'm writing a few pages just to her. I hope she does not forget me as her father.

And now, my darling, let us talk about you. I miss having my arms about you, every minute. We were so close to Winchester, not so awfully long ago, that Geoff and I fought ourselves to remain loyal to our mission. We wanted only to come home and spend but a few hours with you. He is quiet, but so homesick for his Angel.

The fact is, Merriweather, there is a possibility that we may soon be required on a mission that may bring us even closer than we were before. How I shall have trouble then.

I hope the household is well. Give Miss Constance my greetings. I shall pass along a hug (she will protest, but there it is) when I get home.

I have hopes, stronger than ever, that the war will end soon. It makes me fearful to dare to even voice it, but now the likelihood of it happening is strong. It is more than hope now; I feel it in my heart. Soon, perhaps I shall be able to hold you in my arms again and love you as I haven't in a very long time.

Far too long.

As for me, I hate killing and war. I hate feeling as if our brothers—and many of them are just that—are forced to look at us with hatred because of the color of our uniforms. Yet you know as well as I, Winchester has changed hands over seventy times, since the beginning of the war. I could very easily have been wearing a gray uniform, rather than blue, making me an enemy of my dearest friend Geoffrey, with orders to shoot to kill.

Be patient, my darling girl. And be wary. Keep your

weapon near you so that you may be able to protect yourself. How I hate that I'm unable to be there to keep you safe!

Stay out of danger and be vigilant; Watch for soldiers that might try to come and take possession of the house. If that should happen, run to Pembroke as fast as possible.

I know what a huge and loving heart you have, and I also know that you tend to look danger in the face and not see it for what it is.

Be strong and wise, my little innocent.

And behave. Know that I love you with all my heart. I regretfully failed to tell you that once, and I never shall again.

I hope to see you soon.

Your Francis.

MERRIE HELD THE PARCHMENT TO HER HEART AND closed her eyes, tears dripping down onto it. A moment later she picked up the other three and opened them each carefully.

As she finished, she felt a gentle hand on her shoulder, and looked up. Angel had silently entered the room, and came to sit down by her.

"How is Geoffrey?" Merrie's voice was quiet.

"He was well, when he wrote." Angel rose again, and went to the great room door, closing it. "Did he tell you that there was a possibility they might have a mission near home?"

"Yes. But he didn't specifically say they would be able to stop by here."

"No. Geoffrey didn't say that either. But can you imagine either of them being this close and not putting their heads in at home?"

Merrie gasped suddenly. "Francis still thinks I'm at the house! What if he goes there—but the soldier this afternoon said that he didn't think the Confederates were still there.. Oh, Angel, I *hate* this war!"

Angel put her arms around Merrie in an attempt to comfort. "I'm thinking, Merrie, we should keep quiet about the possibility they might come? The children knew there was a chance, and it didn't happen they'd be so disappointed." She sighed. "But Geoffrey did say that he felt in his heart that the war would be over soon. Dare we hope it is so?"

"Yes. Francis said that too. Were you able to read all of your letters?"

"Yes. But I intend to read them once again as soon as I can find a place that's quiet. Perhaps we should return to the dining room before supper gets cold?"

A MOMENT LATER, MIRI SAW THEM COME IN, AND she reached to take the covers off their meals.

"We wanted them to stay warm for you," she explained.

Angel hugged her and smiled. "You have a servant's heart, Miri. Thank you."

"And how are the heroes?" Miri grinned at both of them.

"They are well. And the children will be so relieved," Angel said softly. "I shall gather them together and read the letters to them when I get upstairs."

"Katie will be so happy." Merrie added. "Francis wrote two pages—just to her. I think I'm jealous!" She was laughing now.

Miri looked from one to the other of them, and finally to Nate, as she shook her head.

"I'm so grateful to be here with each of you," she said quietly.

Each of them in turn, smiled back at her, and when she felt a large hand on top of hers, she looked up to see Nate's eyes on her.

A grin covered his face as Nate said, softly, "We're quite fond of you, too, *sassylass*."

ANGEL GATHERED THE CHILDREN TOGETHER THAT evening and read parts of Geoffrey's letter to them. Geoffrey Francis and Nicholas sat there, listening, their faces creased with frowns as she read, and Lizzie was wide-eyed and quiet, so different from her normal dramatic demeanor. But when they left, Angel pulled it out again and quietly read it.

"MY DEAREST LITTLE ANGEL OF PEMBROKE,

I know you have been concerned at the lack of posts for the last two months; it was necessary to keep communication to a minimum due to the nature of our mission. But now I can finally write again. I miss you so, my love, so much more than I can even say with pen on paper. I know when we return from this mission, I shall probably have several of them from you waiting for me.

It was just recently that Francis and I were near Winchester. Can you possibly imagine how difficult it was not to disappear and show up in the middle of the night to join you in our bed? I think about it constantly, and the next mission, it may not be possible to keep from doing just that.

Every curve of your body entices me to disappear, and not even tell Francis where I'm going. He would kill me, of course. He misses his Merriweather equally as much.

How are the children? Please tell Geoff and Nick how utterly proud of them I am. Ask Gracie if she would consider doing another likeness of you all to send me? This one is three or four years old now and is becoming quite worn. Lizzy must be as beautiful as you are by now. I miss them so!

I want you to tell me, my love, how the family finances are holding up? You and Miss Hazel are, I'm sure, keeping a close eye on them. We shall have to reassess things when I return to Pembroke. But we will do what we must. I don't care if we live in a tent so long as I'm with you all. Belongings are, after all, wood, hay, and stubble.

I shall try to write a separate post to the children soon, realizing there are parts of this one you will not wish to read to them. But please tell them this:

I love you all, and I'm eager to gather all of you to me again very soon. You are my pride and joy.

And Angel, know that my love for you remains constant and true. I cannot wait to have you in my arms, just as you're in my heart at this moment.

Be well, my love, and be good. Try your best to stay out of danger. I heard recently there was smallpox near where your location. The soldiers are very aware of it, and at the same time, wary of it. If a soldier were to bring the pock into our regiment it would spread like wildfire.

The posts I'm sending with Private Killian should be safe. He's been a good friend. When we heard he was going home to Winchester, Francis and I decided to catch up and send our letters with him, hoping they won't be intercepted.

*Be safe, my little Angel, and please know how much I
adore you.*

*We hope and pray that the war soon will end, and I may
be with you once again, forever.*

Your loving and devoted husband,
Geoffrey

ANGEL TUCKED THE LETTER INSIDE HER CHEMISE TO
keep it close to her heart, and leaned over onto the
bed, weeping.

17

W *ednesday, March 1ˢᵗ*

WEDNESDAY MORNING, NATE WAS UP AND OUT OF bed, pacing the floor. Miri leaned against the wall with her arms folded, watching him and frowning.

Nate stopped. "You're staring at me."

Her arms remained folded across her chest. "You're pacing. You're going to wear yourself out."

"I want to know what's going on in town."

Miri bit her lip. "How can we find out?"

"I'm thinking." He turned, scowling down at her. "If I leave the house, those here will be in danger."

"Perhaps," she said as she sank her teeth into her

lower lip thoughtfully, "I could go and find out what you need to know?"

"I prefer you not put yourself in danger, either."

Miri's mouth became a straight line. "Nate, I've been going back and forth to town in the carriage every single day," she said, "for five years now."

"Yes, but I didn't love you then."

Miri's sharp intake of breath caused her to choke. Her eyes became large pools of blue as he rushed to her and began smacking her upper back until she could cough.

"Breathe, sweetheart."

She did, finally. "Nate? Could you... please say that again?"

He took her by the shoulders and turned her to face him. "You heard me. I love you, Miri. I cannot bring myself to allow you to go into danger alone."

Miri stood, frozen, staring up into his eyes. She opened her mouth to speak, but her voice seemed to be missing and she closed it again.

"You don't know what to say," he whispered, "do you?"

She slowly turned her head from side to side.

His hands were fisted in her hair, and he brought her face upward as his lips came down on hers. He claimed her mouth possessively; his left arm around her shoulders, and his right at the small of her back.

When his tongue tangled with hers, Miri found herself feeling dizzy. Her breath grew shallow; her heart faster, as she rose on tip-toe and kissed him back. Her knees no longer supported her now, and she barely knew it when the room faded away and went black.

✺

"MIRI?" A DEEP MALE VOICE CALLED TO HER FROM far away. "Miri, wake up, my darling." A sharp tap on her cheek caused her to frown and open her eyes. Her vision still was not clear.

"Pardon?" a whisper answered; she realized it was coming from her own lips. When her focus upward was clear, she realized she was lying on the bed, and he was bending over her closely.

"Miri. Are you all right?" When she nodded, he shook his head. "Good Lord, you scared me half to death! You're never to do that again, you little—" As if he realized he was scolding her, he leaned down to kiss her forehead. "Tell me you're all right."

"I'm all right."

His frown deepened, and he searched her eyes. "Never do I wish to have you pass out on me again. What made you do it? Was I kissing you too harshly? Were you not able to breathe?"

"I think, sir, it was the shock."

"The shock," he repeated. "What shock?" His eyes widened suddenly. "Because I told you I love you? Well, why should I not say it? It's been true since the first day I opened my eyes in the hospital and you were hovering over me. Even then, I wanted you to be mine."

She continued to stare up at him, and he forced her face upward once more.

"Miri, I don't expect you to feel the same. I realize this may be too soon for you—"

"Nate?"

"—and I don't want to pressure you into saying something you don't mean—"

"Nate."

"I understand if you don't, or can't return my feelings—"

"*Nate!*" Her voice was quite insistent this time, and she put a hand over his mouth. "Would you please be quiet and let me speak?"

He removed her hand from his mouth and reached down, gliding his finger across her lips.

"And what, young lady, do you wish to say?"

She pulled his head down to hers until she could reach his lips with her own. Then, softly, she whispered into his mouth, "I love you, too."

Nate wrapped his fist again into her hair and leaned back far enough to gaze down into her eyes.

"I dare you to say that again."

"I love you, Nathan Alley." She breathed. "What? You *dare* me?" Her voice sounded incredulous.

"You heard me."

"Yes, I did. Listen to me, Nate. I cannot deny the feeling I have for you, either. It's impossible."

"Then I have only one question of you, Miri Clarke."

She gulped. "And what—is that?"

"How long will you insist on waiting before I'm able to talk you into becoming *Miri Alley?*"

She gasped and stared.

"Yes," he said, scowling, "I'm asking you to marry me. I know I said I wouldn't, but I can't help myself. Marry me, sweetheart?"

She threw her arms about his neck, and he lifted her off the bed, bringing her lips once more to meet his. "I'm waiting for your answer."

Miri leaned forward. "Yes, Nate. Of course I shall marry you."

"Today," he continued. "Yes, you heard me. Today. We have no promise of tomorrow."

The astonished look on her face changed into one of pleasure. "Today," she whispered.

"Then we shall go to town to find Father Michael.

Then, we'll come straight back. I'll speak with Gleason and Sebastian and see if they can guard the house until then."

IT DIDN'T TAKE LONG TO FIND FATHER MICHAEL. The dormitory turned up empty but for the patients, and Benjamin took them on over to St. Mary's. Miri begged Nate to stay upstairs and let her go down to look for him. Eyeing the steep staircase, he finally agreed, grumbling under his breath.

The ladies were serving lunch to the soldiers. When at last Miri found the Father Michael, he was in the kitchen, helping to ladle soup into the bowls for the soldiers. Handing over his job to Marilyn Thatcher, he followed her up the stairs, groaning at the way his knees complained.

"I need to install a dumbwaiter. These old knees are beginning to say unkind words to me when I insist on taking the steps. Now, my children," he said, smiling, at the top. "How can I help?"

Nate, having found a stool to sit on, waved at him.

"Father Michael, do you need to sit down?"

"Not as much as you do, Captain." A wide grin made its way across his face.

"Well, then, we won't keep you long. Miri and I

desire to be married, and we wondered if you would be so kind as to—"

Father Michael didn't let him finish. Instead, he clasped Nate's hand, shaking it vigorously. "I would be thrilled! When?"

"Today?"

"Today it is. Shall I ride out with Benjamin when he picks up the ladies?"

"That will be perfect, Father. Miss Hazel suggested using the family chapel."

Father looked as if he would dance with delight. He turned to Miri, clasping her hands.

"It's been so long since I had the privilege of performing a wedding. You've no idea just how delighted I am."

"We're excited as well," Nate took Miri under his arm. "And Father, as soon as I'm able, I shall see about installing that dumbwaiter for you."

☙❧

THE AFTERNOON HAD BEEN EXTREMELY EVENTFUL. Angel had caught them on the way back out toward the carriage, and began dancing with glee when they told her about the wedding. She had checked with the others and left early to go home and make further arrangements for them.

The only cease in the chatter was when they passed Merrie's house. Nate's face became grim. Private Killian appeared to have been correct; the Confederates were gone, but the Union Cavalry seemed to have taken their place.

No one mentioned it; Angel continued to chatter all the way home, making plans for the rest of the day, and Miri, looking up at Nate, saw him grinning despite how weary he looked.

"Nate? You look so tired. Please lie down and get some sleep? Everyone else in the house will."

"We shall see, sweetheart." He raised a brow, daring her to argue with him. "We shall see."

But Nate was quite exhausted after the trip to town, and agreed to sleep for a while as Angel dragged Miri upstairs, and sent for Hannah from the staff wing.

"Gracie brought back my wedding gown after she and William married. I believe it might fit you," she said, pulling it out of the wardrobe. A soft knock on the door was heard, and she went to open it.

"Ah, Hannah! We have a bride here in need of your help. Come in!"

"Is it—Miri?" Hannah ran toward Miri and threw fond arms around her neck. "To our captain? This is so exciting!"

"Yes, and Hannah, could you do something with

my hair as well? Father Michael is coming this afternoon to perform it. My hair is clean, but I fear it looks a fright."

It was a busy afternoon. Hannah altered the dress only slightly at the waist, while Angel found the white slippers to go with it. The room was full of chatter as Hannah braided Miri's hair into tiny sections, stopping only long enough to make a trip across to the materials room in the other wing for ribbon.

When she finished, Miri's hair had white ribbons woven into it. Hannah had also managed to find some tulle netting, for a train to go down her back for a lovely headpiece.

Miriam stared into the mirror in tears.

"No, no! Miri, no crying!" Angel leaned forward, kissing her cheek. "You're beautiful!"

"You're so sweet! And I'm so undeserving."

Angel and Hannah both immediately adopted a 'Miss Hazel' stance, hands on hips, stood back.

"*Poppycock!*"

But they realized there had been a third voice added to the mix, and turned toward the door to see Miss Hazel, with her hands on her hips, grinning with amusement. Laughter erupted in the room, and Miss Hazel nodded.

"Father Michael is here. Lady Merrie and Miss

Constance have decorated the chapel, and Lillie is preparing a wedding meal for everyone after the ceremony is over. "We're ready. And Miri, wipe those tears off your face, my girl. It won't do for you to cry your way through your own wedding. Captain Alley is already at the chapel waiting." The bark ceased, and she turned on her heel to leave.

Miri caught her first and raised up on tiptoe to kiss the housekeeper on the cheek. "Thank you, Miss Hazel," she whispered gratefully.

"Hmph." Was the housekeeper's only reply.

But Hannah had a kit out and dragged Miri back into the room. "I have some cover for your cheeks and some rouge and lip color. Be still, now, while we finish."

FATHER MICHAEL STOOD AT THE FRONT OF THE chapel, and when Miri arrived at the door, she forgot to breathe. Nate stood next to him, smiling, dressed in a fresh uniform. He appeared rested, and proudly beamed down on his bride.

Sydney, the only groomsman left in the stables aside from Sebastian and Benjamin, raised his violin and began to play the wedding march.

Miri stood in awe as she glanced around the

chapel. For the next few moments the war seemed to go away. There was only her handsome and happy Groom and the chapel of ladies there. The decorations on the pews were beautiful, and the sound of Nate's voice and hers as they recited their vows in the hushed atmosphere of the small chapel, she would never forget.

Miri stuttered slightly as she nervously began her vows, and paused.

Nate, however, sensed her embarrassment and smiled down at her. He reached down to touch her cheek, whispering, "Take your time, sweetheart."

A deep breath later, she smiled and recited them.

Cheers and applause broke out inside the chapel. Gracie and Ellie, who arrived home just in time for the wedding, came running to her to hug her. Everyone allowed Nate to escort her back toward the house.

On the way back, however, Miri glanced toward the family graves, and Nate saw it.

"Come with me, sweetheart," he murmured softly into her ear as he led her toward the plot and stopped. "Which grave belongs to Burton?"

Miri took his hand as she led him toward the snowy grave. There were still a few Easter daffodils blooming through the snow, and she leaned down to pick one.

Side by side, they stood there as Miri took a few moments to speak to Burton. She kissed the small flower and placed it gently on his grave.

Nate took a step forward. "I promise, Burton," he said humbly, "I'll do my utmost to take good care of her."

He seemed to be in no hurry to go as Miri smiled up at him, but wrapped his arms about her to warm her.

She turned toward Nate finally. "I'm ready, Nate," she said. Nate nodded, urging her back to the house. She clung to him as he turned with his back to the winter wind to protect her.

The dining room was decorated and beautiful. Her dream continued to be perfect as they sat down. Lillie and Miss Hazel brought in a meal that was only slightly fancier than their traditional evening meals, but at the end Lillie brought in the four-layer cake she had decorated and frosted that afternoon. It was complete with tiny roses and looked exquisite. Lillie served the first piece to Nate and Miri before serving the others.

Nate, noticing that Miri seemed quiet, reached under the table to grasp her hand.

"Are you all right, sweetheart?"

She smiled as she raised shining eyes to his. "Yes, Nate. I'm very happy."

The smile he returned warmed her.

"Now," Miss Hazel said from the doorway. "As soon as the cake is eaten, Sydney has agreed to provide some music in the formal Ballroom for dancing."

Excited chatter broke out as everyone moved into the Ballroom. Miri knew they were giddy with delight at having dancing in the house again.

Father Michael stood at the end next to Sydney, a wide smile plastered across his face.

"I wish you to know, ladies, however rusty I am in the Ballroom, I would be happy to dance with every single one of you beautiful ladies. But first, I believe Captain Alley and Miri should begin."

Sydney glanced at Miri for instruction, and she smiled, "A waltz please, Sydney?"

"Thank you, little Miri," Nate smiled down appreciatively.

"I wanted to avoid something that might be too strenuous, sir." She said, grinning upward into his face.

The others joined in. Even Cissy and Polly were downstairs, giggling as they danced with each other and showed their most dramatic flair.

"Oh, my dear, what a lovely evening this is," Polly feigned a near faint by putting the back of her hand to her forehead. "Is it not?"

"Of course it is, you dolt," Cissy said, giggling back. "How often is it we get to dance in the midst of this horrid war?"

Miri, unable to help herself, looked up at her husband. He turned toward the twins and chuckled.

"Ladies, you look lovely this evening," he said with a wink.

Polly pretended the beginnings of a swoon, and Cissy giggled, pulling her twin sister off the dance floor. "I do so wish Abel was here to dance with us. Or Geoffrey Francis."

"Well *I*, for one, *don't*," Polly groaned. "They are upstairs, acting the soldiers on duty. Not a bit of fun in them."

Nate turned toward Miri with a huge grin.

"You, Mrs. Alley, are extremely beautiful. Have I told you that today?"

"No, Captain, I don't believe you have. And so are you."

He scowled. "Beautiful?" His expression was of blatant disbelief. "Watch your mouth, little girl."

A tinkling little laugh escaped. "No. I meant, you're quite handsome."

"Better. I should not wish to have to deal with you here on the dance floor."

Another giggle came from Miri, and he raised a brow. "She giggles," he muttered under his breath.

"But I must admit, it sounds delightful." He pulled her against him, and she leaned her cheek against his chest, closing her eyes. Nate tucked her head beneath his chin and held her tightly.

IT LASTED ONLY A FEW MOMENTS. MIRI GLANCED up, seeing Sebastian standing in the doorway to the kitchen. An expression of concern covering his face.

When Nate led Miri to the door and approached Sebastian, he leaned forward. "Abel has been watching from the upstairs windows, Captain. He thinks he may have spotted some figures in the shadows, approaching from the North, by the pond."

Nate nodded toward Sydney, who stopped playing. Silence reigned over the gaiety as he spoke. "I hope there is no need for alarm, ladies and gentlemen, but it appears we have some visitors attempting to approach from the north."

"Shall we fetch our weapons, Captain?" Miss Hazel asked.

"Yes, I believe so, Miss Hazel. I apologize, everyone."

No one complained. Within a few moments, Nate had gone for his rifle. Miri had the pistol Burton had given her, also at the ready. She still wore the wedding dress and long headpiece, along with her slippers.

The lights were extinguished now and the house was extremely quiet. The boys were at their posts, watching the windows, and the ladies were each at their places of watch.

Every person in the house was ready. Miri sighed quietly as she glanced around.

The war was back.

silence broken...

IN THE DARKNESS, THE HOUSE GAVE AWAY NO secrets as to what was happening. They waited tensely, listening for any signs of attack. But the only sound they heard was the lonely chime of the grandfather clock.

Suddenly, Abel's voice was heard from the top of the stairs.

"The garden gate outside the kitchen is breached!" he called out, as loudly as he could.

All hell broke loose. Nate, forgetting his chest,

ran toward the kitchen as he heard a scream from Lillie.

The sound of "Shh" was heard, and Miri called out. "Nate? *Nate!*"

Just as he turned back to her, two large figures assaulted him from behind. Nate collapsed to the floor, and Miri screamed at the top of her lungs, running toward her husband.

Every figure in the house had their weapon aimed and ready to fire, but knew they couldn't, for fear of hitting their captain. And now Miri was in the middle of the fray. She jumped on the back of one of the assailants, screaming as they pounded on her husband.

"Stop! *Stop it!* You'll kill him!"

Gracie jumped in next. She grasped the collar of the waistcoat of the other and pulled backward, and Angel grabbed onto an outstretched arm just before it made another strike.

"Let him go!" Gracie screamed.

"What?" a voice said in the darkness. "*Miri?* Gracie?"

Merrie was pounding on one of them now, screaming, "Stop it. *Stop!*"

"Damnation, Merrie—get off me!" A voice said.

"No! Leave him alone!"

"Wait! *Wait!* Everyone, stop, *now!*" Angel cried,

loud enough for everyone else in the house to hear. "Bring a lantern!"

A lantern moved from around the corner in the hands of Miss Hazel. It took a moment before she was close enough to make a difference.

Angel peered in at the two men and stood up straight, her hands on her hips. "Geoffrey Wellington!" Her voice was fused with fury. "Get off of him! Francis, you too!"

Francis and Geoffrey stared at each other as they halted. Miri was pounding on them now, pushing them off of her husband.

"Damn you, Francis and Geoffrey! If you've hurt him..."

Merrie was tugging Francis away from the pile of bodies. "Francis Adams," she said, her innocent little voice full of anger, "If you have hurt our captain, I swear I shall never speak to you again."

Geoffrey allowed Angel to tug him backward. But he was still staring at Francis in confusion. Then, suddenly he turned and grasped Angel by the shoulders. "You, young lady—explain. *Who* is your captain?"

The houseful of ladies all began talking at once in a cacophony that shook the household. No one could hear anyone else as they all spoke at once.

"*Someone tell me*," Francis' voice bellowed above all the others, "*What the hell is going on here!*"

Silence.

"Lower your voice, Francis Adams." Merrie's voice. "There are children present in this house. We shall explain." Merrie's innocent voice had taken on an uncharacteristic sternness.

His brow rose. "Please do." He said, his own tone quite stern now.

Geoffrey's voice was next. "And I want to know," he said, "just what has happened to this house! We hear music and dancing and laughter from the outside, and sounds of celebration when there is a war going on? And I come into my own home to hear screams, and to find a strange man in here, but when we attempt to save you from him, all of you are furious. And now you are referring to him as *your captain?*"

It was Miri's petulant voice that answered. "Keep your voice down, Lord Geoffrey. He's trying to wake up. The lantern here, please?" She was opening the waistcoat of Nate's shirt, praying that he hadn't begun to bleed. The others began to scurry as she barked orders, indeed sounding rather like Mollie. "Angel, bring fresh bandages and some iodine. And bring the light closer this way, please. Thank you Miss Hazel."

The household became utterly quiet as Miri removed, one by one, the bandages that covered Nate's chest. Tears streamed down her face the longer he went without speaking.

"Nate? Nate, *please speak to me! Please!*"

His eyes opened suddenly, and he glared up at her. "Miri? What in damnation happened? My chest feels like a *A silence broken...*

THE HOUSE, IN THE DARKNESS, GAVE AWAY NO secrets as to what was happening. They waited tensely, listening for any signs of attack. But the only sound they heard was the lonely chime of the grandfather clock.

Suddenly, Abel's voice was heard from the top of the stairs.

"The garden gate outside the kitchen is breached!" he called out, as loudly as he could.

All hell broke loose. Nate, forgetting his chest, ran toward the kitchen as he heard a scream from Lillie.

The sound of "Shh" was heard, and Miri called out. "Nate? *Nate!*"

Just as he turned back to her, two large figures assaulted him from behind. Nate collapsed to the floor, and Miri screamed at the top of her lungs, running toward her husband.

Every figure in the house had their weapon aimed and ready to fire, but knew they couldn't, for fear of hitting their captain. And now Miri was in the middle of the fray. She jumped on the back of one of the assailants, screaming as they pounded on her husband.

"Stop! *Stop it!* You'll kill him!"

Gracie jumped in next, grasping the collar to the waistcoat of the other and pulling backward, and Angel grabbed onto an outstretched arm just before it made another attack.

"Let him go!" Gracie screamed.

"What?" a voice said in the darkness. "*Miri?* Gracie?"

Merrie was pounding on one of them now, screaming, "Stop it. *Stop!*"

"Damnation, Merrie—get off me!" A voice said.

"No! Leave him alone!"

"Wait! Wait! Everyone, stop, now!" Angel cried, loud enough for everyone else in the house to hear. "A lantern!"

A lantern moved from around the corner in the hands of Miss Hazel. It took a moment before she was close enough to make a difference.

Angel peered in at the two men and stood up

straight, her hands on her hips. "Geoffrey Wellington!" Her voice was fused with fury. "Get off of him! Francis, you too!"

Francis and Geoffrey stared at each other as they halted. Miri was pounding on them now, pushing them off of her husband.

"Damn you, Francis and Geoffrey! If you've hurt him..."

Merrie was tugging Francis away from the pile of bodies. "Francis Adams," she said, her innocent little voice full of anger, "If you have hurt our captain, I swear I shall never speak to you again."

Geoffrey allowed Angel to tug him backward. But he was still staring at Francis in confusion. Then, suddenly he turned and grasped Angel by the shoulders. "You, young lady—explain. *Who* is your captain?"

The houseful of ladies all began talking at once, in a cacophony that shook the household. No one could hear anyone else, as they all spoke at once.

"*Someone tell me,*" Francis' voice bellowed above all the others, "*What the hell is going on here!*"

Silence.

"Lower your voice, Francis Adams. There are children present in the house. We shall explain." Merrie's innocent voice had taken on an uncharacteristic sternness.

His brow rose. "Please do." He said, his own tone quite stern now.

Geoffrey's voice was next. "And I want to know," he said, "just what has happened to this house! We hear music, and dancing and laughter, from the outside, and sounds of celebration, when there is a war going on? And I come into my own home to hear screams, and to find a strange man in here, but when we attempt to save you from him, all of you are furious. And now you are referring to him as '*your captain*?'"

It was Miri's petulant voice that answered. "Keep your voice down, Lord Geoffrey. He's trying to wake up. The lantern here, please?" She was opening the waistcoat of Nate's shirt, praying that he hadn't begun to bleed. The others began to scurry as she barked orders, indeed sounding rather like Mollie. "Angel, bring fresh bandages, and some iodine. And bring the light closer this way, please. Thank you Miss Hazel."

The household became utterly quiet, as Miri removed, one by one, the bandages that covered Nate's chest. Tears streamed down her face the longer he went without speaking.

"Nate? Nate, *please speak to me! Please!*"

His eyes opened suddenly, and he glared up at her.

"Miri? What in damnation happened? My chest feels like a Minie' ball went through it."

Miri began to sob, relieved that he was awake and speaking, and he reached up, fisting her hair in his hand and pulling her down to his chest. "Shh. It's all right. Don't cry, little one."

Father Michael spoke up, trying to gain the attention of Geoffrey and Francis. "Lord Geoffrey, Sir Francis, I believe I can explain. If you will follow me into the great room, please."

"Father Michael?" Francis' voice cried in disbelief. "What the hell are you doing here?"

"Francis!" Merrie scolded. He turned to her, then to Father Michael, realizing he'd just cursed in front of the priest. Meekly, he added, "My apologies, Father. I'm still quite confused."

"Understandable, my son. Follow me."

Both men scowled at him and followed as their wives stayed to see how the captain was.

"Is he all right, Miri?" Angel asked.

"I hope so," Miri whispered, with a sob. *"Dear God, I hope so."*

Nate took her chin in his hand. "I'll be fine, sassy-lass. All it did was take the wind out of me. Now, will you finish my bandage so I can get up?"

Miri stared at him and threw her head back in

delighted laughter. All the ladies in the room began to laugh with glee.

"The captain... the captain is all right." Female voices said with relief. "He's going to be fine."

Miri carefully changed the bandages. There was no active bleeding, and she placed fresh bandages across the wound. Hannah picked up the soiled ones to dispose of.

It was then that Nate looked around at the sea of relieved faces staring down at him. He smiled at them, and then up at his wife.

"And now, my girl. I need to get up."

"I believe we need to go into the Great room and meet Lord Geoffrey and Sir Francis," she said, as he pushed himself slowly up and off the floor.

"Yes." He agreed, wrapping an arm around her for support, groaning as she tugged him upward.

"Are you certain you're all right, sir?" Miri's voice was filled with worry.

"No worries, Miri. I'm fine," he answered. "*And I desperately need to sock someone in the mout*h."

GEOFFREY WAS THE FIRST TO STAND WHEN MIRI walked into the great room at Nate's side. He held out a hand.

"It seems I owe you a monumental apology, my friend. I had no idea that you were here to protect our families at Pembroke. Francis and I came into the back door and suddenly heard screaming and mayhem, and we erroneously assumed that you, not we, were the cause of it."

"Nathan Alley," Nate put out his hand. But he was not smiling.

"First Lieutenant Geoffrey Wellington."

Francis followed. "Captain Francis Adams. I understand you're a Captain, as well."

"Discharged," Nate scowled. "Due to bullet wounds."

"He's still recovering," Miri was scowling as well, looking from Geoffrey to Francis. "You could have killed him."

Nate reached down to pull her to him. "Enough, Miri." He said in her ear. Then he looked toward the two men in front of him. "We're on the same side. They did what they perceived to be right, in trying to protect their homes and families."

Miri looked up to see that his brow held warning, and lowered her gaze. But she was still wearing a frown, even though she didn't speak.

Geoffrey grinned at Nate. "Miri will forgive us eventually. We hope, Captain, we didn't do any lasting damage. It will be dreadful if we have."

Nate answered grimly. "I believe I'll live."

Geoffrey nodded. "I'm quite relieved to hear it." He turned, glancing around behind him. "Where is my little red-haired volcano?"

"I'm here, Geoffrey," Angel's voice wafted into the room from the doorway.

"Ah. There you are, my love. Come upstairs with me and let me see the children. Francis and I can't stay long, but we couldn't be this close without seeing you." He turned to give a smart salute to Nate as he guided her toward the stairs.

Stopping at the foot, he lifted her into his arms. "It's been a long time since I carried you up these steps," he whispered into her ear.

Angel threw her arms about his neck. "I've missed it so," she whispered back.

Francis once again reached out to shake Nate's hand before raising it again in salute. "Geoff is right. We can't stay long. Where is my girl?" He looked around him.

Merrie's cough caused him to turn. "Francis Adams, if you dare to leave this room without me, I shall never speak to you again. And how did you know I was here? At Pembroke?"

Quickly he whirled around to see Merrie, and a wide grin spread across his face.

"We passed the house first, and realized the army

had taken it. It was a matter of deduction. Then I knew you would be here. And as far as deciding not to speak to me, I believe that's the second time you have threatened me with that." He picked her up and whirled her around, and proceeded to throw her over his shoulder.

"Francis! Put me down!"

"Oh no. Never." But he stopped, turning back at Nate. "You, sir, are in charge of the house. Have I permission to take my wife upstairs for a bit and see my daughter?"

Nate smiled for the first time. "Absolutely, Captain."

But they heard Francis muttering as he carried Merrie toward the door.

"So you refuse to speak to me, hm? Well, my little miscreant, it doesn't matter one whit. What I'm about to do to you does not require conversation."

"Oh? *Really*, Francis." Merrie's laugh followed.

As Miri watched them go, she looked up into her husband's eyes. "You're very forgiving, sir. I'm still angry."

"Miri, I'm fine. While I appreciate your devotion, it's time to let this evening's episode go. You and I shall have years of time to spend together. These men must go back into service and finish their mission. This war is not yet over."

She sighed. "I suppose that's true," she said, frowning. "But I'm so glad you don't have to go back into battle."

The household was gathered in the ballroom when Nate strode back in with Miri under his arm. The clock struck one-thirty as they entered.

Miss Hazel approached. "Should we stay on alert, Captain?"

"I wish I knew, Miss Hazel. Where is Abel?" He glanced toward the top of the steps.

"I'm here, sir." Abel's young voice met his ears as he stepped around the corner.

"Could you and Geoffrey Francis take a good look and tell me if you see anything at all? The moon is up. We shall check on the front and back from here if you can look from upstairs."

Hannah and Gracie ran in one direction; Miss Hazel and Sebastian the other. Father Michael went yet another to watch out the windows for shadows, while Nate and Miri went to peek carefully out from the great room windows. They met together a few moments later.

"It's clear from upstairs, sir," Abel reported.

When everyone else reported in, Nate nodded thoughtfully. "I believe it would be all right for us to get some rest, ladies and gentlemen, but keep your weapons close by and be ready, please. I shall watch for a while from down here."

Sebastian stepped forward. "Captain, I can take your watch from down here. You're injured, and you just married. We would be happy for you to rest for a while."

"I will join him," Father Michael added. "I'll go upstairs and keep watch with Abel and Thomas."

Nate said a grateful word of thanks, but when it came time to leave, he couldn't bring himself to have others on watch while he slept. He stayed downstairs, watching, and pulled Miri to his side.

"Lean over and rest on me a bit, sweetheart. I'm accustomed to these watches."

She didn't argue, but did rest against him with his arm wrapped securely around her. Despite the present threat, she felt safer than she had in years. She wondered just how long they could stand to sit awake night after night. Sheridan's army was supposed to be gone southward by now, but how could they know?

And where was Friberg?

IT WAS FOUR A.M. WHEN A SHOUT FROM ABEL awakened the household once more. "Soldiers approaching from the road and east from the bridge. A mass of them."

The house sprang to life once again. Miri sat up straight, taking a few seconds to realize what was happening. Nate, next to her, shouted an order to stay where she was and moved toward the window, as Geoffrey and Francis came barreling down the staff staircase and in from the kitchen, each in various stages of dress.

Nate stood, fully awake and erect, and called out orders. "Thomas—Abel, see that the younger children are safely hidden. Constance, see to the children in the staff wing. Geoffrey, man the east side. Francis, the front. Father Michael, watch from the 3rd story—Sebastian..." He continued calling out orders. "And ladies—keep the ammunition coming if you can. But *stay down!*"

Just then, the front window shattered.

Miri, still in her wedding dress and slippers, stood to her feet. Nate grabbed her and pulled her to him, bending her over backward and kissing her mouth passionately, before saying, "Bring ammunition, sweetheart, but stay down. *And away from the windows*! I don't want you fighting—let us do it."

Miri watched as he started forward, about to protest, but closed the door again and went for the ammunition he would need. There was no way she would abandon him.

"Nate," she whispered after him, "you have no idea how much you mean to me."

The window in their bedroom blew out into the room in a myriad of pieces as she entered, and she fell to the floor to take cover.

How dare they?

The anger inside her turned to fury. She pulled up her skirts and crawled toward the window, ignoring the glass that lay on the floor. Within seconds, she saw a wall of soldiers moving toward the house, over the bridge. She peered through the broken window and fired, then fired again. She watched as they halted and backed up. Had they thought there would be no retaliation?

Miri was reloading her pistol as another shot came through the window, and rose up far enough to shoot again, and then again. A horse reared, and she saw that soldiers were falling to the ground. There was gunfire from other windows on this side of the house. Geoffrey?

"Miri!" It was Gracie's voice, and she turned.

"Gracie, there are too many this way; they will be here in just—" she paused as she fired another shot, "a moment."

Gracie aimed, beside her, and fired six shots in rapid succession, out the window.

Miri stared at her. "It shoots six?"

"Yes." She nodded, handing over another gun. "*Here*. This was another one of William's. It's loaded."

Miri took it and emptied it toward the soldiers that were halted now. It gave her enough time to reload while Gracie moved to the next window and began shooting again. But the window above her shattered, sending glass into the room. Gracie looked down to see blood dripping onto her hand, not realizing where it was coming from, until Miri gasped.

"Gracie! You're injured!" Before she thought about what she was doing, she had picked up the hem of the dress and wiped the blood from Gracie's forehead.

Both of them looked down, and said simultaneously, "Well, damn." But Gracie immediately began to reload her weapon, while Miri did the same.

"I've ruined Angel's wedding dress! She'll hate me!" Miri muttered.

"No, she'll hate *me* for bleeding all over it." Gracie threw back.

Miri moved back toward the first window and emptied her weapon once again. Shots were coming from the upper floors now, and she heard Angel's shout from the open upstairs window, and an occasional answer from Merrie. Ellie and Betsy were most likely shooting from upstairs, too.

Miri wanted desperately to go to the great room and check on Nate, but was hesitant to leave Gracie. The soldiers weren't shooting toward the windows as much now; they seemed to take a turn on this side of the bridge and were going around toward the front of the house. There were still so many.

Miri crawled toward the bed. "Gracie!" Miri called out. "Help me get the footlocker to the great room."

They both ducked under the bed on their knees and tugged it outward. Miri crawled back to the wardrobe to get the extra rifle, then followed Gracie into the hallway and across toward the great room, shoving the footlocker forward.

"Nate?" It was Francis' voice; he was in the great room now, positioned next to Nate. "You'll tear your chest open using the rifle." But when he turned back to see Gracie with William's six-shooter, he smiled and held out a hand. "Here, Gracie. Nate needs that one."

"Here." Gracie shoved it toward him, along with the ammunition, and he handed it to Nate. Miri handed hers to Francis.

In a few seconds, Nate leaned up over the windowsill and fired; six soldiers fell. The glass was missing from the big window, and Gracie crawled toward the stairway. A moment later, she reappeared with another firearm and a heavy box of ammunition, and pushed it toward them.

Miri took the six-shooter from Nate and reloaded it as he fired, using the other.

Nate ducked below the window and grabbed Miri, pulling her down lower. "I believe I told you, young lady—"

"Don't you dare scold me, Nate. You need me here." She handed him the extra gun while she loaded the others. There were gunshots coming from almost every outer room in the house now and Miri wondered how much ammunition they had left.

She heard Nate whisper. "I don't know about this, Francis. There are so many."

The room was getting lighter, and Miri looked around. First light had passed; the sun was coming up. She looked up to see Nate's worried face. Francis had slowed down on his firing now and turned to look toward them.

"Nate? How much more ammunition is there?"

"There *was* plenty," Nate answered, looking back toward the empty lockers behind them. "But we didn't expect a shelling such as this. I honestly don't know. The Union Cavalry was what we expected. This seems to be an army."

"Here." Geoffrey picked that moment to crawl up behind them, dragging several three more lockers. "But this is all there is left. It must have been distributed to the rest of the house. I hope Father Michael is asking God for a miracle."

They, along with Miri and Gracie, began reloading their guns. But there seemed to be a silence momentarily.

Francis raised his head and quickly ducked back down.

"Damn."

Nate stared at Francis. "What did you see?"

"Enough."

"Are they blue or gray?."

"It's not light enough to tell for sure, but gray, I think."

Geoffrey had not stopped loading, but spoke under his breath to Nate. "Nate, let me take over for a while. You need to rest."

But Nate shook his head. "No, my friend. My loved ones are here, too."

Miri's heart fell as she looked up at Nate. He reached out to touch her face gently; almost, there was a hint of sadness in his eyes.

Then he turned back toward the window, and once again took aim.

THERE WAS ONE LOCKER OF AMMUNITION LEFT. Geoffrey had moved over toward the piano, which was riddled with glass and bullets now. The firing from upstairs had lessened.

Suddenly, the gunfire from the outside ceased. Fear, palpable, hung in the air. So did the silence.

Francis, Nate, and Geoffrey exchanged glances as they waited.

Miri looked up at Nate. What was that she heard? Horses' hooves? Nate reached back and pushed Miri behind his back to protect her, and Gracie moved behind her. Each of them had a fully loaded weapon in their hands. Another set of hooves was heard; then another.

Shouts rumbled through the army outside, but only shouts; there was no gunfire. The bedlam that erupted with its dissonance and clamor had each of them inside staring at each other and wondering what was happening.

"Do you hear?" Nate whispered. He held up his hand to silence the others. "Listen!" he whispered. "It's a retreat."

Geoffrey and Francis stared. The sound of horses moving toward the road grew fainter, until there was only dead silence.

They waited, unmoving, in case it was a trap. No one spoke. The light outside was brighter now.

The clock struck six.

Someone began descending the stairs from the family wing, and footfalls were heard from the floor behind them.

They each turned around to see Father Michael approaching. "I've been on the third floor watching their faces, my children. I must see what they were looking at. No—don't get up. I haven't been in the middle of the firing as you have. Let me at least do *this*." Slowly, he approached the foyer and unbolted the front door as the others watched and waited.

They heard the door creak as it opened. Only silence followed.

Still, they waited. Suddenly they heard a chuckle from Father Michael, which erupted a moment later into a full-blown laugh. They heard him bolt the door. By the time he approached the door to the great room he had thrown his head back in a belly-laugh he couldn't control.

Miri kept an eye on Nate. He was sitting back, as was everyone else, eyeing the priest as if he had indeed lost his mind.

"This, ladies and gentlemen of Pembroke," said Father Michael, "is the miracle we prayed for. This is what caused the soldiers to cease firing, and leave the premises in such angst." He walked toward them, pulling something from behind his back.

He handed it to Nate who also began to laugh. He held it out to Geoffrey, and one by one they passed it around.

It was a piece of artwork; a stick figure clearly drawn in a child's hand with a round face that frowned back at them. The face was dotted with spots, and under it there was writing in large print.

"Quarantined: The Pock is here."

19

T *hursday, March 2nd...*

NATE OPENED HIS EYES WHEN THE CLOCK STRUCK nine. The rest of the household was once again beginning to awaken. They had all fallen asleep in the exact places they'd been when Father Michael entered, bearing the sign Cissy and Polly made, declaring the household had been stricken with Small Pox. By the time they realized that the two mischievous twin girls had saved the household with one piece of paper, they'd been so exhausted no one had bothered to move.

Hearing footfalls on the stairs, Nate turned.

Angel and Merrie had come downstairs on quiet tiptoe to find their husbands sound asleep on the floor amidst an overabundance of glass. Angel smiled as she noticed Nate had pulled Miri into his arms with her head up on his shoulder. There was blood everywhere on the white wedding dress. But she was sleeping soundly, curled up in her husband's arms.

Gracie was the only one who had moved over onto the tapestry rug and gone to sleep with her head resting on the pillow she had pulled from a chair. There was a bit of dried blood on her face, but not a lot.

Nate glanced around, seeing Father Michael seated on the steps. The priest was right. The genuine miracle was that no one in the household was badly hurt. A few scrapes and bruises, and cuts from the shattered windows could be treated easily.

The tapping of Miss Hazel's cane was the next sound Nate heard; she'd come into the great room, likely to tell them breakfast was ready. She opened her mouth to speak as she glanced at Nate, but as she took in the scene, she smiled at him.

When she turned to leave, she raised her cane off the floor and left without a sound.

It wasn't until ten o'clock that Miri stirred. She glanced into her husband's face, and he drew a gentle hand down her cheek. Next, she glanced over at Angel, who now had Geoffrey's head resting in her lap, and smiled. Motioning silence, Angel put a finger to her lips and grinned.

Francis, however, was mumbling in his sleep. Merrie was perched over him, kissing his face lovingly and encouraging him to awaken. When he finally opened his eyes and saw her, a huge grin plastered its way across his mouth. Uncaring whether anyone was watching, he grabbed her and brought her head down to his, kissing her in delight.

He got to his knees, suddenly, and pulled Merrie to her feet.

"And now, little brat," he said into her ear, uncaring if the others heard. "I'm taking you to bed."

"Take my room," Gracie said, giggling after them.

Geoffrey was awake now and watched as Francis carried Merrie up the stairs over his shoulder. Turning toward Angel, he leaned down and kissed her forehead. "Well, my love, you heard the gentleman. And I cannot leave until he does, so... come with me." He laughed at Angel's scarlet face and reached down once again, picking her up in his arms. He held her closer, kissing her on the way to the stairs.

Miri's gaze moved to Nate as he took a handful of her hair, combing through it with his fingers.

"Your hair is still full of glass, sweetheart," he murmured quietly.

Miri reached upward. "Is it?"

He smiled. "I'm amazed the ribbons have managed to remain in place despite the siege." He paused, smiling. "And one more thing."

Miri glanced up, waiting until he spoke again.

"As a married man, I have yet to experience the delights of my wife. And *I*," he added, tilting her head upward, "shall not be denied any longer."

Nate rose to his feet and pulled Miri up beside him, taking her hand before turning back to Gracie. He paused at the door. "We shall be back in a while, Miss Gracie."

She only smiled. "Go, Captain."

But Ellie's's voice wafted through the open dining room door, and Nate paused to listen. Ellie sounded full of disbelief. "Father Michael, you cannot be serious."

"Oh, but I am, Miss Ellie. Quite," Father Michael answered. "And before you scold either of them for going outside the house to plant this well-done and well-thought-out sign, consider the fact that they saved every single person in the house from being massacred. I believe they both deserve a medal of honor."

Nate and Miri both moved into the dining room far enough to witness the scene. Ellie and Miss Betsy were both staring at the sign, but looked up at them when they heard footfalls. Gracie had preceded them in.

"Where is everyone?" Ellie asked, looking past Nate and Miri to Gracie.

"Oh, if you mean all the lovebirds," Gracie said, her eyes twinkling, "I'm sure I wouldn't know... but —" she paused when Father Michael rose from the table, "Father Michael? Please stay with us?"

"Thank you, Gracie, but I believe I must get back to town. And I promise not to tell a soul that Geoffrey and Francis were here. All of you need to rest today. I shall see if I can scare up some good people from the parish to help at the hospitals in your places. Please tell Geoffrey I enjoyed using the Chapel yesterday afternoon. If I could, I would take it with me. A shame it is so far from town." He winked at them. "As for now, I plan to tell Miss Hazel and Lillie thank you, before asking Benjamin to take me back to St. Mary's."

Gracie observed him as he left by the back door toward the stables. "And," she said, giggling as she sat down to eat, "Ellie, you asked where all the lovebirds were. I can't say for sure, but I would strongly advise staying away from Angel's room. And Miri's room. And Captain Alley's room." Glancing band and spying Nate and Miri, she put a hand to her mouth. " Oh, there you are, Captain. Sorry, Miri."

Miss Betsy put her hand to her mouth. "Gracie!" she chuckled, "What would William say if he heard you say such a thing?"

Gracie chewed her lip thoughtfully. "He would probably scold me," she said, grinning with mischief. "And oh my goodness, how I miss that!"

❦

NATE, EAGER TO BE ALONE WITH HIS BRIDE, LED Miri into the bedroom and closed the door, turning her to face him. Bringing her face upward and taking her mouth with his, he kissed her once; then twice more. She looked up, seeming a little shy, and he guided her toward the bed. But the first thing he noticed was the chilliness of the room. He halted, staring at the bed. It was covered in glass; some of it bloody. Miri's wedding dress was covered in blood, and it wasn't the first time he'd noticed it. Now, however, it captured his complete attention.

"Miri?" His voice held such a tone of alarm, he

felt her immediately tense. His gaze moved from there to the window, where the eastern sun gleamed in on the few jagged panes of glass that remained. The curtains were completely gone, along with most of the glass. From there, he looked to the floor, where much of it had landed. Blood spatters were prevalent on the floor and the wall. Bullet casings littered the floor.

He glanced down at Miri with eyes that he knew were stern; hers were quite wide. His hands were on her shoulders as he held her away from him and looked her up and down, scowling.

Miri, too, was looking down and gasping in dismay. The blood on Angel's wedding dress was everywhere; on the bodice and below it; the elbows. The lower layers were not only bloody, they were ripped.

"Oh! Angel's dress! In the dark, I didn't realize."

But Nate gave her shoulders a slight shake. "It's not the gown I'm concerned with, young lady. Turn around."

She blinked, but obeyed, as he unfastened the buttons down the back of the dress. Once, she sneaked a glance back at him, and he paused. When her eyes met his, she turned quickly away, looking as if she was going to cry.

Nate brought the top of the dress away, and drew each of her arms up to study them. They were cut and bleeding. He scowled with dismay and then brought the rest of it down to her ankles, helping her to step out of it.

A breeze came through the missing window, and she shivered. Nate knew she had to be cold. He threw back the coverlet on the bed and brought her down to sit on the edge of the sheet. But when she shivered again, he retrieved a woven wool throw from the corner of the room and shook it out, wrapping her in it and pulling her into his lap.

"Let me look at you." He reached down and examined her hands and elbows, then her knees. They were worse. He shook his head and lifted her chin, forcing her eyes to meet his.

"Did I not tell you to stay away from the windows? It is quite obvious you disobeyed me."

Her eyes were downcast.

"Miri? Answer me." He couldn't keep the anger out of his voice; and she choked out a small sob.

"*Yes.*" Tears trickled down her face.

"Did you hear me when I instructed you to take cover and not to fight?"

"Yes.*"

"Did you choose to disobey me intentionally?"

She shook her head.

"Sweetheart, when I ask you a question, I want you to answer me aloud."

"No, sir. Not intentionally." But he barely heard her answer.

Nate couldn't help himself; he pulled her to his chest tightly. *"Dear God,"* he whispered into her hair. *"What am I going to do with you?"*

"I'm sorry I disobeyed, Nate. But you needed me, and I knew it. I couldn't abandon you."

"Were Francis and Geoffrey not there with me?"

"Yes, but——"

"I wasn't abandoned, Miri. The only reason I wasn't wild with worry is because I thought you were obeying me. I had no idea you were in here on your hands and knees crawling about and shooting out the window."

"I'm sorry."

"What do you think I should do about this?"

Sadly, her eyes rose to meet his. "I don't know."

A small knock on the door caused Nate to scowl. He wrapped her more tightly in the throw and looked toward the door. "Yes? Come in."

It opened. Hannah had a tray in her hand, but before she spoke, she looked around at the wrecked room. "Oh my. May we come in and clean this up for you, Captain?"

Nate looked down at Miri, and nodded his head.

"That would be much appreciated, Hannah. Miri is hurt. I'll take her into the bath and bandage her up while you have someone do that."

She set the tray down and closed the door again. Nate stared down at his wife.

"This is serious, Miri. I fail to see how I can just let this go. But first, come with me into the bath and let me work on your wounds.." He set her down on her feet and led her into the bath. Before she realized what was happening, he lifted her to sit on the top of the table by the sink.

She gasped. "You should not be lifting me, sir."

"You're not heavy. Be still, or I shall add swats to your sentence."

Gently, he began to take a cloth and wash the glass from her hands, elbows, and knees. A few pieces of it still remained, and she grimaced as he cleaned them. She whimpered a few times, and once, he stopped, frowning down at her. When he began once more, he was gentler.

As he finished, he opened the door to the bath. The staff had almost finished cleaning up the glass and the blood. A blanket hung over the window, but the room was still cold.

Hannah nodded to him. "Miss Hazel said there is a room on the other side of the wing on the third floor, sir, that has no damage and is unoccupied. If you would like to move up there it's ready, now."

Nate nodded. "We shall move up immediately, Hannah. It's too cold to keep Miri down here. Please tell Miss Hazel thank you. And you need not bring meals to the room. We shall come down." He smiled, and she nodded, and left.

Nate returned to the bath and opened the door, to see that Miri was leaned over against the mirror, her eyes closed. She was trembling and looked miserable. He approached her and wrapped her in his arms.

"Sweetheart, we're moving to the third floor. It's too cold down here for you. Are you able to walk, or do I need to carry you?"

"No—I wish to walk," she said, hurriedly. "You can't carry me—it's too much."

"Then you may. I have changed my mind about your punishment. You've been through far too much today already." When she looked up with grateful eyes, he eased her down from the table and supported her as much as he could.

"Lean on me, Miri." He murmured.

She made it up to the second story, and was halfway to the third when she stumbled. Nate immediately leaned down and picked her up in his arms.

"Here, sweetheart," he kissed her forehead, and she leaned her head on his shoulder. "Lean on me. I have you."

Hannah met them, turning down the bed in the room, and motioned him in. "The bath, Captain, is through that door, and private. The public bath adjoins it on the other side. You should have privacy. There is a hot water bottle at the foot of the bed for warmth. The fire is going, and I brought the food tray up here. The lantern is here on the table. And sir —about tea?"

"Don't hold it for us, Hannah. Unless we're needed, we may sleep through the rest of the day. But I shall try to get Miri to come down for supper. Thank you so much for all you've done."

"Yes sir. Please call if you need us."

Nate watched as she closed the door, and tucked the blankets in around Miri, in the bed. The fire was crackling away in the hearth, and the room was toasty and warm. He thought of the house he owned in Fredericksburg, and wondered if it still stood, while he removed his waistcoat and breeches, and climbed in behind Miri, curving his body around hers. She whimpered, but instead of pulling away from him, she snuggled backward against him and sighed softly.

The warmth she created eased the ache in his chest, and he smiled. From the corner of his eye, he could see the tray of food waiting, but decided against it.

He needed nothing right now as much as he needed Miri against him. Smiling, he closed his eyes.

And slept.

⚜ 2 0 ⚜

 wakening...

A SINGLE GONG FROM THE CLOCK ON THE MANTLE caused him to open his eyes. He squinted at the mantle. Five-thirty. It was almost dark. Was it a.m. or p.m.?

A sigh from Miri in her sleep reminded him where he was. So much had happened since their wedding ceremony, yet he still hadn't been able to take her in his arms and make love to her. The fire-light was still casting shadows; he wondered if someone had come in while they were asleep and stoked it.

Forcing himself to move, he had to admit he felt rested for the first time in a very long time. He didn't know where his clean uniform was, but managed to find the waistcoat and trousers on the chair and tug them on. He lit the lantern and looked over at Miri, watching as her face flickered in the firelight. She was still asleep.

"Sweetheart," he said, leaning over her, "it is time to go downstairs and eat. I know you may not want to, but you need to. Wake up."

She looked up; her eyes squinting in the lantern light. "I'm not hungry."

"Perhaps, but you need to eat. Come. Up you go." He was reaching for her, and she frowned as he sat her up on the side of the bed. Nate stared down into her face. "How do you feel this evening?"

"It is evening?" She sounded confused.

"I think so. And I don't wish to have you late for supper. And.." he looked around the room, "I have no clue where to find your clothes in order to dress you. The wardrobe?"

"They may still be in the room where Gracie is. Wait—they changed our rooms, didn't they?"

"We're on the third floor of the staff wing. Stay where you are."

A knock from the door brought Nate to answer it. Gracie stood outside. "Miri needs something to wear. Here's a gown for this evening. Then I shall set her things out, and have them brought over after supper. This is for now." She handed over a pale green gown and some undergarments.

MIRI GRUMBLED THE WHOLE TIME NATE WAS dressing her. But when he popped her bottom with large hand, she looked over her shoulder at him and became quiet.

They were downstairs just in time. The other girls were already seated, and were chattering away.

Angel smiled as she greeted them. "We're surprised to see you two. We figured you would be as tired as we are."

Nate was the first to answer. "Miri and I wanted to check on everyone and see if there has been any unusual activity today."

Ellie, from across the table, looked toward them. "Sebastian said that he saw two soldiers on the road in front of the house. But he said they didn't even venture a glance this way, and just kept going."

"I hope that's good news," Merrie said, yawning. "I'm in no mood for another siege tonight. We could all use a good night's sleep."

Nate looked down at her. "I suppose Geoffrey and Francis went back?"

"They left about noon. But it was so wonderful to see them." Merrie's eyes twinkled. And they both got a wonderful lunch from Miss Lillie before having to leave. Katie was so thrilled to spend some time with her father."

"The boys and Lizzy were too," Angel added. "But I'm jealous, Merrie. I had to share Geoffrey with three children, instead of just one." But she was laughing.

Miri looked toward Gracie, sitting on Ellie's other side. "You're quiet, Gracie," she said, softly.

Gracie glanced at Miri. "Umm... have you shown Angel the dress?"

Miri was about to shake her head when Angel laughed. "I've seen it. Well, the dress has seen better days. Hannah worked on the stains, but in the end, we decided to make bandages out of it. Don't fear, Miri. It served its purpose. I wore it; so did Hannah and Carrie and Gracie, and now, you. I'm very pleased."

"Oh, Angel," Miri's sigh was a sad one. "I'm so sorry—I knew I had ruined it forever. I had tried to be so careful with it, and then when I walked in the bedroom for ammunition, they blew out the window."

She caught Nate's expression as he put a hand over hers.

"You *walked* into the room?"

The gravity in his voice caused them all to freeze.

"Um.. yes—but fell to the floor as soon as the window shattered... sir." She hoped that the added "sir" would derail the displeasure his face so clearly showed.

It didn't.

Supper was quiet after that. Everyone tried to lighten up the mood in the room with their chatter. But Nate, although he thanked Miss Hazel and complemented them on the food, said little, and Miri said almost nothing.

Nate turned to Miri, after she had stopped eating, and glanced at her plate.

"Are you finished, sweetheart?"

She nodded, and he took her hand, guiding her to stand.

"Excuse us, ladies. It was delightful. Please, once again, give Miss Hazel and Lillie our compliments."

Gracie stopped him as he began to turn Miri toward the door. "Have you any idea what to do about tonight, Captain Alley? Do you think they will come back?"

"I doubt very much they will. At least the ones who saw the sign on the door are unlikely to, and word travels quickly. If they believe we have the pox here, they'll stay away."

"Geoffrey put the sign back up before he left, Captain," Angel said, softly. "If it helped this morning, perhaps it would again."

"Perhaps. A good idea. Ladies, unless we're needed before then, we shall see you in the morning."

Miri looked up into his face as he led her from the room. She heard Angel's voice as they left.

"Uh-oh."

MIRI STAYED SILENT ON THE WAY UP TO THE ROOM. Nate's face was grim as they ascended the steps. He looked down into her eyes as he closed the door and led her over to the side of the bed.

"Come here, young lady."

She went. Her voice trembled as she spoke. "You're a-angry with me."

He led her over to stand in front of him. "And what makes you think so?"

"Are—are you not, sir?"

"I'm angry with what you did. I'm not angry at you. Do you understand the difference?"

Miri felt her eyes widen, but shook her head slowly. "N-no, sir."

"You must never think I don't love you. But you must learn when I give you orders for your safety, it's never acceptable to disregard them. This was one of those instances. Your behavior was unacceptable, but only because it put you in danger."

Her gaze lowered, and he lifted her chin. "Do you understand me, Miri?"

"I think so."

He stared down, frowning. "Now. I'm going to ask you a question. And please answer me honestly. I shall know if you lie."

She waited.

"I think it's time."

She swallowed hard and waited. She was waiting for the word 'discipline' to escape his lips. "Nate?" She asked, "what are you going to do?"

"I know this isn't what you need right now," he said, gazing downward into her eyes, "but it's what I feel both of us has need of. I'm going to kiss you. And cuddle you, and be intimate with you. But I need to know if you feel well enough."

Surprised, Miri looked up. "I'm well enough." Her voice was trembling. "But it's you I worry about. Please—*please* don't hurt yourself, sir."

Nate held her, his hands on her shoulders, and folded her close to his chest. He was still watching her closely when he stopped suddenly, staring down into her eyes. "Miri." When she looked up, Nate lowered his mouth onto hers, invading with his tongue. "*I want you*," he whispered into her mouth.

She stared up into his dark and dilated eyes as something began to stir deep inside her. "Yes, Nate," she whispered, "I want you, too."

His eyes glittered in the lamplight, and the gold in the center was showing; not with anger now but with desire. Miri stared up into them.

Nate smiled. "Your eyes are a deep indigo now."

"Nate?" Her voice may have sounded uncertain, but she wanted him; she knew it. The depth of her own passion surprised even her. "Take me?" She whispered. "N-now?"

The smile that widened across his handsome mouth evoked a deep response once again.

"I shall, in my own time. Patience, my love."

She couldn't relax, but tried to keep still as he unfastened her gown.

Nate began at her neck, slowly unbuttoning each tiny button one at a time. She felt his lips following his fingers downward each time he pulled the gown away. Then, slowly, he tugged it down and dropped it to the floor. Next he unfastened the cords over her corset, letting it follow the gown. As he came to her undergarments however, he leaned down and began a pattern of kissing up her thighs toward her bottom.

He ran his hands along her body and she stared downward, eager to know what he would do next. She moaned, wishing suddenly he'd never stop. She was slightly disappointed when he raised her to her feet and turned her to face him.

"Hands behind your back, little girl," he ordered, softly.

She obeyed, watching him with wide eyes.

Nate began boring into her deep blue eyes with his. He leaned forward, kissing her forehead, and then removed her chemise. Next, he gently rubbed his thumb over the open spot. The second kiss was on her left cheek; the third, her right. The next kiss came as he loosened the chemise and ran his hand downward, tracing the area between her breasts gently.

She shivered. His next kiss was on her mouth, as he moved his tongue inside once again.

"Don't faint again on me, little girl," he teased, "or you shall awaken to me planting swats on that delicious little bottom."

She took a deep breath, determined to stay with him. "Surely you would not dare to spank me for fainting, sir."

His brow rose. "Try me."

"But—" She got no further before his mouth silenced hers. But now the chemise had followed the corset, and she stood naked, before him. "Nate," she gasped.

"Yes, my darling?"

"I..." she took a deep breath; it was spastic and she felt as if she was not getting enough air.

☙❧

"MIRI?" A VOICE SAID, FROM FAR AWAY.

Her eyes fluttered open. She moaned. His voice was next to her ear now, and she struggled to look up at him.

"Are you all right, sweetheart?"

She nodded.

"Am I going to have to revive you every time I kiss you?"

"No—but Nate..." she cried out once again as the world faded.

A moment later she awakened to him blowing lightly across her ear.

"I believe your body likes this whether you do or not. And beware, little girl; this is not *all* I intend to do to you. Trust me?"

"I trust you," she whispered,. She was pleading as her eyes met his, and he pulled her backward and began pressing her downward into the pillows.

This time she held on. She didn't move, but

followed him with her eyes as her shattered world slowly began to return to normal. She heaved a deep sigh, looking up into his face.

"Ah," he said, smiling. "But I'm still not quite finished with you." He refused to take his eyes from her as he leaned forward once again.

How long she was out this time, she didn't know. But when her eyes fluttered open, her breathing was somewhat ragged. Nate's face was inches away and obviously concerned.

Slowly, she leaned upward and kissed his mouth. "I'm all right, Nate. It is just so..."

A grin spread across his mouth. "So?"

"So intense, sir. "But please don't stop. I love what you're doing." She took a deep breath, her eyes wide.

"Trust me, sweetheart, and never doubt me; I shall not stop." He paused, leaning down to kiss her ever so gently before saying,

"You're mine, Miri Philippa Alley. All mine."

EPILOGUE

E *pilogue*

"THE WAR IS OVER..."

IT WAS APRIL. THE WAR HAD ENDED FOUR DAYS earlier, when General Robert E. Lee, the leader of the Confederate Army, had surrendered at the courthouse at Appomattox, to General Ulysses S. Grant. Celebrations had broken out in the county as the soldiers began to arrive home from the war to be reunited with their families.

Slowly the soldiers from the hospital were

released from their beds to begin their journey home, and St. Mary's and the dormitory began to empty out.

Nate took Miri to town every day to care for the wounds of the remaining soldiers while he helped them make preparations for their travels home. Dr. Foster welcomed them both, since they no longer quarreled as much.

A week later, the last of the soldiers left for home. Miri stood in the doorway of the parlor for a long time. "The dormitory is to be a dormitory once again as soon as Louisa returns," she murmured. "Angel will be pleased."

Nate wrapped his arms around her. "And the war," he said softly, "is over."

⚜

THAT AFTERNOON, NATE ESCORTED MIRI BACK TO Pembroke. As they moved inside the drawing room, Miri stopped abruptly and stared.

The blue crystal lamp was once again sitting on the table by the piano, in front of the window.

"Angel?" Miri smiled. "It's back!"

"Yes!" Angel was staring, her arms folded, at the lamp. "I brought it out of hiding this morning as soon as they replaced the window. I thought it was time to put it back in its rightful place."

"It's beautiful," Miri said softly.

"Isn't it? I can't wait for Geoffrey to see it when he gets home. Of course, he's not as fond of it as I am, but..." She paused, looking up as she heard James open the front door.

Gracie flew into the room, her fists clenched and her eyes blazing. "My house," she fumed. "You should see my house! They've left it in a state of ruin!"

Miri put a hand to her mouth. "Oh, Gracie, I'm so sorry."

"Well, perhaps ruin is too strong a word, but I ran all the way up to the second story where William built my studio. And you won't believe what I found."

Angel moved to put her arms around Gracie's neck. "I'm sorry too, Gracie."

It was then Miri spotted William, standing in the corner of the room, and waved at him as she hugged Gracie.

Gracie, however, wasn't in the mood for hugs. She allowed a quick one from Miri, and then stood back, her temper still raging.

"*Hell's bells*! Miri, you should see what they did to it! How can they sleep at night! I hope they all burn in—"

But Miri silenced her by holding up a hand. "Um, Gracie?"

"What!"

Miri pointed a finger at the corner of the room, just behind the fuming Gracie, who stopped. Her cornflower-blue eyes grew wide as she stared at Miri and then Angel, and blinked. She gulped and suddenly began to turn very slowly around to look behind her.

"I believe, young lady," said a deep voice, "we've had quite a few discussions regarding your language."

It was William.

Miri couldn't help but notice the longing on Gracie's face as she gazed at her husband for the first time in several years. "Oh, William," she whispered, "you... you're taller than you were when you left."

"Am I?" William seemed to be attempting to keep his gaze forbidding, but his eyes betrayed his amusement.

"Yes..." Gracie ran, jumping into his arms and kissing him with wild abandon. "Oh, William! I'm so happy to see you! It's been so long!"

He gathered her closely in his powerful arms, laughing. But the others could hear him as he spoke in her ear. "Oh yes, Gracie Becker. Apparently It's been too long. It appears yet another discussion about your language is in order. Right now, however, I believe you should bid our hosts goodbye for a little while."

Gracie turned sheepishly back to Angel, then Miri and Nate.

Before she could speak, however, Nate grinned. "I believe it's time for Miri and I to go upstairs. But William, it's nice to meet you, and we shall be eager to have you stay at Pembroke until your house is repaired. I'll be glad to come over and help. Come, Miri."

Miri gave Gracie a sympathetic glance as Nate herded her up the curved staircase. "Poor Gracie," she breathed.

"Poor Gracie, you say? Miri, that young woman needs exactly what's coming to her. No, so help me, young lady, don't you dare to argue with me. You know it to be the truth."

❦

THE NEXT MORNING...

It had been a long day. Now that the last of the wounded soldiers were gone, Miri helped Hannah at the dormitory, preparing it for use once again. Nate was stronger now and helped as they moved furniture, mopped it out and cleaned it thoroughly. They applied a coat of wax to the floors, tables and furniture, putting everything back into place. Nate had spent much of the day whitewashing the shared room.

By the end of the day they had replaced the curtains with new ones, and set the desk back in its usual place. Hannah was almost finished making matching coverlets for the beds. Even the artwork had been replaced. By the end of the week, it should be ready for use again. Then they could start work on the church hall at St. Mary's.

Nate turned toward Miri and Hannah. "Ladies, you've worked yourselves to a frazzle today. It's time to go home."

Hannah nodded. "I believe, Captain, you're right. But we aren't the only ones who worked hard. So did you."

Nate smiled and nodded. "The war is over, Hannah. Please, just call me Nate."

She smiled as she got into the coach and leaned back. Miri followed, and Nate closed the door, nodding to Benjamin.

They glanced out the window as they approached Pembroke.

"How many times have we made this trip in the last five years?" Miri said softly.

"Too many, my love," Nate answered quickly. "Entirely too many."

Hannah eyed them, smiling. "Yes. Indeed."

No one else spoke as Benjamin pulled in through the circled drive in front. Hannah was the first to step out of the coach when they arrived. But Nate kept Miri inside, noting the extra horses that were out in front of the house.

"It seems we have company, sassylass."

"It does, indeed. You don't recognize the horses because it was dark when they were here before, but I do."

Nate gave her an odd glance as he escorted her in through the front door, pausing as he heard the commotion from the great room. Several male voices, some familiar and some unfamiliar met their ears, along with the voices of children. Miri turned toward it and ran inside, tugging Nate along with her.

Geoffrey and Francis were standing in front of the window, staring at the new glass that covered it, and looking over the piano. It was still riddled with bullet holes and looked fragile, at best.

Another gentleman was standing there, looking it over with dismay. Ellie stood next to him, her arms as far around him as she could reach. Cissy and Mary Polly were wrapped around his legs, and Thomas also stood by as closely as he could. His father's hand rested on his shoulder.

"You must be Henson Andrews," Nate said, saluting. "Major."

Henson returned the salute with a grin. "And you must be Captain Alley. Indeed, and call me Henson. Geoffrey and Francis were just showing me how you brought such mayhem into the house." His wink at Miri was met by her surprised eyes.

Miri's surprise turned into fury as she stared at him.

Ellie too, was appalled at his comment. "Henson Andrews, I'm quite ashamed of you! How *dare you*!"

But Miri's outraged, "Excuse me?" interrupted, her voice raised enough so they could hear her all the way back in the kitchen. "Henson Andrews, that is the *biggest statement of bullsh*—"

But she got no further. She gasped as Nate's hard hand connected with her bottom.

"I believe you know better than that, young lady," Nate said into her ear. "Upstairs with you. *Now*."

But Francis, a twinkle in his eye, nodded his head. "Oh yes, it was the truth," he said, grinning. He moved forward until he was standing directly in front of Nate.

Geoffrey, appearing highly amused, moved in as well. "As God is my witness," he added, "it certainly is. Mayhem cannot come near describing it—"

It happened before either of them knew it was coming. Nate sent one fist flying against Geoffrey's jaw; the other toward Francis'.

Geoffrey was thrown back backward, and bounced toward the table next to the Queen Anne chair, dislodging the beloved blue crystal lamp. It immediately hit the floor and shattered across the room. Francis, on the other side, landed against the damaged piano, knocking loose the leg. He rolled out of the way just in time to avoid the instrument as it came crashing down, sending dissonant sounds of music throughout the house.

Both men were lying on the floor now. Geoffrey was rubbing his jaw as Francis pushed himself upward, shaking his head. Angel came rushing into the room to see what was happening.

The first thing that caught her eye was her husband on the floor trying to get up; the second was the blue crystal lamp, scattered in tiny pieces across the floor and sending prisms of blue into the room.

Angel began to lecture him furiously. "Geoffrey Wellington! That was the lamp your mother sailed with all the way from England! It even managed to survive through five years of war until now. *How could you*! You..." But she stopped abruptly in the midst of her tirade. Staring at the blue crystal in bits all over the room, she seemed to have frozen in place.

"The lamp," Miri said in dismay. "The blue crystal..." The room held only silence as she stared from one person to the other.

Geoffrey moved quickly to Angel and put his arms around her. "I'm sorry, my love. Truly."

But still Angel only stared. A few seconds later, she brought both hands to her face, covering it. Francis and Geoffrey exchanged glances, as if wondering if she'd lost her mind.

Tears were running down Angel's face now, as she stared from Geoffrey to Francis. "What happened?" She asked finally.

Geoffrey scowled toward Nate. "He hit me."

"I did, and I apologize, ma'am," said Nate. "It's all my fault."

Angel looked from one man to the other, and suddenly began to howl hysterically with laughter.

"Captain," she said, "no apologies needed. It's about time you were allowed revenge for the night our husbands attacked you. And besides," she added, "the lamp was only wood, hay and stubble. It's time I stopped worrying about it."

Merrie was on the floor, rubbing her hand over Francis' injury. But as soon as she realized he was all right, she smacked his arm hard, and began to scold him in her innocent little voice. "Look what you've done, Francis Adams. That poor piano! For shame!" Her fist drew back in preparation for another strike.

Francis caught her arm, and immediately put one hand on the back of her neck, the other over her mouth, scowling down at her. "You, you little miscreant, are in deep trouble." Then, rising to stand and pulling her up with him, he turned to Nate. "I swear, Captain," he said, checking the growing lump over his cheekbone. "Did you ever think of taking up boxing?"

Nate was shaking his hand as if to get the feeling back in it. "No," he said, "but I must tell you, Lady Wellington is right. After the way you two attacked me the last time you were here, this makes me feel..." he stopped, glancing at the children, and then turned back to them, silently mouthing, "*damn* good."

"*Nate!*" Miri squealed, her voice raised in rebuke. "Shame on you!"

Geoffrey and Francis both held out a hand to Nate. Ellie now had her head thrown back, laughing, and Mary Polly and Cissy began dancing around their father in delight at all the commotion. Thomas merely watched his two younger sisters, shaking his head in admonishment.

Geoffrey's deep laugh joined everyone else's. "My good man, I believe we had that coming. And Francis is right. Gentleman Jackson would have been honored to have you as a successor."

"Ah, but I have no intention of boxing," said Nate. "My goal is to take my bride back to Fredericksburg to see if my house is still standing. If not, I think we shall have to build another one." He paused. "And depending on how many people still reside there whom I know, we may well decide to come back and build it here." He turned back to Miri as his face grew stern and leaned over toward her. "And I believe, young lady," he said in a quiet but stern voice, "I said *upstairs with you*."

Miri seemed to know he meant it. She turned to obey, as Francis passed her, going through the doorway with Merrie thrown over his shoulder. "Quiet, Merrie Lynne." He was saying softly, not caring if Miri and Nate could hear. "I believe you know what happened the *last* time you tried using those little fists on me."

Geoffrey passed them next, carrying Angel, who was squirming in his arms, trying to get down. His voice also seemed to be intended only for his wife's ears, but Nate and Miri clearly heard it. "And you, my love, know better than to try to scold me in front of others. No, don't deny it. You know you have this coming."

Henson was next. He smiled at Nate and Miri as he led Ellie and the children toward the stairway. "I believe the children have some studies to finish this afternoon." At their groans, he turned to his wife, urging her along with a hand to the small of her back. "And I believe you and I have some things to 'discuss' as well, sweetheart."

Miri looked up at Nate, her expression confused.

"You hit Sir Francis and Lord Wellington," she said. "Why did you not hit Sheriff Andrews?"

"He outranks me," he said simply, as he pulled her into his arms. But leaning down he whispered, "And as soon as I get you alone, my darling, you'll find yourself sorry for your language. Come with me."

Miri stamped her foot, trying to pull free of his arms. "But that's not fair. *You* said—"

"I know what I said, young lady. But I didn't say it aloud, in front of a roomful of children." He threw her over his shoulder, just as Francis had Merrie a moment earlier, and when she struggled, he smacked her bottom hard, with his hand. She squealed, and another smack followed the first.

Carried over his shoulder, Miri looked down as he climbed the staircase with her. The room looked almost as bad as it had the morning after the Union army had tried to confiscate the house. Even then, however, they had left with the piano intact.

Angel's poor piano. It would likely would never be the same again, and the lamp she had worked so hard to preserve was in tiny shards all over the room.

Miri couldn't remember the house being so full of destruction.

The last thing she saw, however, was Miss Hazel coming into the great room from the hallway. She paused in the doorway, looking it over with dismay. The blue glass cast prisms over the remains of the piano, reflecting now off the remains of the chandelier.

Miss Hazel stood there a moment, staring at the room. Then, putting her hands on her hips, she shook her head.

"It appears I only *thought* the war was over," she muttered, turning and disappearing back into the kitchen.

"Hmph."

THE END

ABOUT THE AUTHOR

Pippa Greathouse is the author of around 40 books; ranging from historical fiction to FBI, Police Procedurals. She also writes FBI mysteries and cozy mysteries under the name Tessa Carr and some under the name Gracie Griffith.

She comes from a large family active in law enforcement, which is partly responsible for her interest in writing in this particular field.

Pippa has several other books out that are Historical Fiction; some are in the process of being rewritten and recovered (and republished).

This particular series, *The Damsels of Shenandoah County*, contains five books that will take you from the year 1843, to the end of the Civil War, in 1865. While every effort is made to keep the facts accurate, all the characters and their lives are completely fictional.

Enjoy!

The books in this series:

Lady Angel of Shenandoah County (1)

Lady Merriweather of Shenandoah County (2)

Ellie of Shenandoah County (3)
Gracie of Shenandoah County (4)
Miri of Shenandoah County (5)
Abby's Keeper
Christmas of Iron and Lace
Poker and Promise

Written with Ruby Caine:
Conquered by the Captain (1)
Conquered by the Commander (2)
Conquered by the Ghost (3)
The Rough Edges Series:
Rough and Honorable (1)
A Rougher Touch (2)
Rough and Noble (3)

By Tessa Carr :
The Shadows of Council Creek Series:
Faces in Shadow (1)
Danger in Shadow (2)
Screams in the Night (3)
Blood Spatters Don't Lie (4)
And from Gracie Griffith:
The Soul of Benjamin
And many others which are in the process of being rewritten, recovered, and re-released.

Milton Keynes UK
Ingram Content Group UK Ltd.
UKHW020051181024
449757UK00011B/590

9 798227 650986